DRUNK GIRL

LYRICS AND LOVE SERIES
BOOK 2

SAMANTHA LIND

SAMANTHALIND.COM

Drunk Girl
Lyrics & Love Series Book 2
Copyright Samantha Lind 2019
All rights reserved.
Print ISBN: 978-1-956970-30-2

No part of this publication may be reproduced, transmitted, downloaded, distributed, stored in or introduced into any information storage or retrieval system, in any form or by any means, whether electronic, photocopying, mechanical or otherwise, without express permission of the publisher, except by a reviewer who may quote brief passages for review purposes.

This book is a work of fiction. Names, characters, places, story lines and incidents are the product of the author's imagination or are used fictitiously. Any resemblances to actual persons, living or dead, events, locales or any events or occurrences are purely coincidental.

Trademarked names appear throughout this novel. These names are used in an editorial fashion, with no intentional infringement of the trademark owner's trademark(s).

The following story contains adult language and sexual situations and is intended for adult readers.

COVER DESIGN BY *MELISSA GILL DESIGNS*
COVER IMAGE BY TAYLOR ALEXANDER PHOTOGRAPHY
COVER MODELS TABITHA AND SCOTT WILSON
EDITING BY *ALL ABOUT THE EDITS*
PROOFREADING BY *PROOF BEFORE YOU PUBLISH*

 Created with Vellum

DEDICATION

To all those who believe in second chances. The ones who want to give up but dig deep and find themselves in the process.

"You can't go back and change the beginning, but you can start where you are and change the ending." C.S. Lewis

CONTENTS

PLAYLIST

Drunk Girl ~ Chris Janson

1

NICK

"What can I get you?" I ask the patron who just took a seat across the bar from me.

"Blue Moon. Slice of orange, if you've got it."

I reach for an orange to slice for his beer. "Short or tall pour?"

"Tall sounds good," he says, looking at his watch. I grab the glass and fill it with beer, adding the slice of orange before I set it down on the coaster in front of him.

"Did you want to open a tab?"

"Sure, you got a menu I can take a look at?" he asks before taking a drink.

"Absolutely." I grab a menu from the pile behind the bar. "Just flag me down when you're ready to order."

I step away, looking out over the bar I own with my brother, Kaiden. We've poured our blood, sweat, and tears into this place over the last five years, making it what it is today.

It's Thursday night, which is ladies' night, so I anticipate the crowds will start rolling in, in about thirty minutes or so, as more and more people get off work. The bar scene in our part of Nashville is steady. The city has poured a ton of money into revitalizing this section of town, and it's why Kaiden and I picked this location when we were ready to open. The city was subsidizing new local businesses that were willing to invest in the area and help breathe life into it. With that backing, it allowed us to purchase this building rather than pay a landlord rent. It was a moneymaker for us from the first day, since we have other units within the building who rent from us.

I wipe down the bar, tossing the bar rag over the sink before I fling the dry one over my shoulder. I stand back, watching as people start to trickle in, filling up the tables as they meet up with friends.

"Order up," Katie, one of our best waitresses—who also happens to be my sister-in-law as of about six weeks ago—says as she approaches the end of the bar with her cocktail tray and starts punching in an order on the kiosk.

"How's it going today?" I ask her as I start filling the beers for her order.

"Good. How's it going for you?"

"Can't complain. Another day, another dollar," I

tell her, handing over the last of the four beers in her order.

"I hear ya." She grabs four coasters and the beers, and heads over to her customers' table, where a group of rowdy guys cheer as she sets down their drinks.

The night picks up from that point as the after-work crowds start to pour in. Between the food our kitchen puts out and the large assortment of beers we have on tap, we've become one of the more popular bars on our block. We feature live music, which on its own isn't special—it's Nashville, after all—but for the area of town we're in, we've made a name for ourselves. We're the neighborhood bar for the crowd looking for that laid-back atmosphere, but also the place the mid-twenty to mid-thirty crowd goes to for a good time, without having to go down to lower Broadway where all the famous bars are.

As I wipe down the bar for the hundredth time tonight, I watch patrons finish off drinks and leave. I'm vigilant about making sure people aren't leaving drunk then getting behind the wheel. If push comes to shove, I'll personally pay for someone's Uber or Lyft ride to get them home safely, if they can't get one themselves. I turn to put away my rag when I notice a young girl at one of the tables in the corner. She looks almost lost. Not plastered drunk, but she's definitely had a few drinks tonight. The group of girls she was with earlier has left, leaving her behind and by herself.

I keep my eye on her as I go through my nightly

checklist. She's in no condition to be driving, so I leave the bar and head over to her table, bringing a glass of ice water with me.

"Do you have a ride home?" I ask, setting the glass down on the table in front of her. She lifts up her head, her bloodshot eyes meeting mine. It's then I realize she's crying. *Fuck.* I don't do well with girls who are crying, they're kind of my kryptonite.

"Yeah, sorry. I was going to call an Uber." She pulls her cell from her purse. "Fuck," she mumbles.

"What's wrong?" I ask, taking in her appearance. She's casually dressed, in shorts, a tank top, and cowgirl boots. A normal ladies' night dress code for many of the women who come in here.

"My phone is dead. I can't order the Uber without it," she says, showing me the black screen of her iPhone.

"I've got a charger behind the bar. I can take it and plug it in for you for a bit. You're welcome to stay here or move over to the bar."

"Thank you," she replies, the tears that were falling just moments ago now drying up. She slides out of the booth, grabbing her purse and phone, and follows me over to the bar. I take her phone and plug it in next to the register.

"Would you like anything from the kitchen before they close down for the night?" I offer, sliding her glass of water in front of her that I carried back over to the bar. "My treat," I add as an afterthought.

"That's so kind of you," she says, holding back a new flood of tears that are threatening to spill from her lashes. "I'd love an order of the nachos, if that's not a problem."

"Regular or supreme?" I ask, pulling them up on the computer.

"Supreme, please."

"Chicken or beef, or both?"

"Chicken, no jalapeño, and extra sour cream, if you don't mind."

"Not at all. Anything else?" I ask before I send the order to the kitchen.

"That's all. Thank you." She picks up the glass of water as I step away and grab the broom to start sweeping the floor behind the bar. I'm able to get that done and have just finished stacking the floor mats that need a good cleaning into a pile, to mop the floor beneath them, when the mystery woman's order is brought out.

"One order of supreme nachos, with chicken, no jalapeños, and extra sour cream." I repeat her order as I set the platter in front of her, along with a roll of silverware and a few extra napkins.

"Thank you," she says, digging into the platter.

"Anytime. I'm Nick, by the way."

She accepts the hand I've offered across the bar. "Ashley."

"Holler if you need anything. I'm going to start

mopping while you eat and your phone charges for a little while longer."

"Will do," she tells me.

I busy myself filling the mop bucket with water and floor cleaner before I get to work on the area behind the bar, followed by the non-slip mats that cover the area. With all that done, I head out into the open area of the bar and start helping Katie flip the chairs up on the tables so we can clean the floors out here. We've been working together now for a few years, and have a pretty good routine down.

"How was the food?" I ask Ashley when I return behind the bar to check on her.

"Just what I needed. Thank you."

"Anytime," I tell her. "You looked like you could use something to cheer you up."

"Yeah," she says, emotion filling her voice. "It's been a pretty shitty day, that's for sure."

"I'm sorry to hear that."

"I got laid off from my job, only to return to my apartment to find my boyfriend fucking a girl he works with."

"Shit. That *is* one hell of a day."

"That it was." She pulls her hair out of the ponytail it was in and readjusts it to gather all the flyaway hairs that had fallen out.

"Do you have someplace safe to go to tonight?" I ask, then wonder what the fuck I'm going to do if she tells me no.

"Yeah, my mom just lives across town."

"Good. Here's your phone. It's up to fifty percent, so it should last you for a while."

"Thank you," she says, accepting the phone from me. I see her hit the Uber icon and go through the process to set up a ride. "My ride should be here in just a few minutes. Thank you again for the food and water. I really appreciate it."

She slips off the bar stool and heads for the front entrance, watching out the windows. Her ride pulls up outside not too much later, and I watch as she walks out to meet it, sliding into the back seat.

"Ready to lock up?" Katie calls out to me from across the bar, pulling my attention from the taillights disappearing down the road.

"Yep," I tell her, now that it's only the two of us, besides the few employees still cleaning and shutting down the kitchen.

Thirty minutes later, the kitchen staff has all gone home and Katie and I are packing up, as well. She only has to go up the stairs to the upper penthouse apartment she and Kaiden share.

"Goodnight. Thanks for all your help tonight," I call out as I lock up the back door before walking out to my truck.

"Night, Nick!"

"See you on the flip side."

2

ASHLEY

I REST MY HEAD ON THE SEAT BACK IN THE UBER car, the events of today rolling through my memory like a movie reel. I swear, if it weren't for bad luck, I wouldn't have luck at all these days. I've bounced from dead-end job to dead-end job, and obviously didn't learn from my mom's mistakes when it came to picking the men I date. I can't fucking believe Chris was fucking that slut.

I squeeze my eyes shut, willing the reel from today to stop playing on repeat. I thought going out with my friends would help put me in a better mood, but really, it only masked things for a few hours. It also didn't help I couldn't really afford to be out at a bar. Without a job as of today, and now an apartment, either, my life is really in the dumps. Moving back in with my mom will have to do until I can find another job and save enough to get a small apartment of my own.

"We're here," the driver calls from the front seat. I open my eyes, looking around at the rundown apartment building my mom has lived in since I was a teenager.

"Thanks," I say before opening the door and sliding out. I walk up the cracked sidewalk and push open the front door that, at one point, used to lock, but hasn't in at least five years. I walk down the dimly lit hallway to my mom's unit, passing by Mr. Richards' unit, where his television is loud enough I can tell exactly what show he's currently watching on some cable news station. The old man is one of the sweetest people I've ever met, but damn, does he need to get his hearing checked.

I rap my knuckles against the door before I slip my key into the lock and open the door. "Mom," I call out as I step inside. "Mom, it's me," I say, a bit louder. I can hear voices coming from down the hall, so I know she's here, and apparently not alone.

"You fucking bitch!" I hear a man's voice yell out, and then the telltale sound of skin smacking skin. I run for her bedroom and bust through the door, where I find my mom's latest boyfriend standing a foot or so away from her as she cradles her cheek. The one he's just backhanded or slapped. I can see the skin already puckering and turning red from the contact.

"Get the fuck out of here before I call the cops!" I yell at him, the adrenaline taking over. I've seen this scene one too many times to allow it to go on.

"Who the fuck are you?" he snarls.

"Her daughter, that's who. And I said to get. The. Fuck. Out," I seethe as I grind my teeth together.

He scoffs. "Whatever. I'm outta here." He turns and beelines it out the door.

"Mom," I say, turning back to her. "What happened?"

"He didn't like something I said," she replies, blowing off what just happened.

"You can't just take this shit from these men, Mom. You deserve better," I tell her before I go find her a bag of frozen peas to ice her swollen cheek.

She settles on the couch and flips off the TV while I take a seat on the recliner on the other side of the small living room.

"What brings you by so late?" she finally asks me, breaking the silence that had fallen between us.

I let out a big breath, stalling for a few seconds before I answer her. "I had a pretty shitty day. Got fired, then walked in on Chris fucking some chick, so I left. Ended up going out with a few friends for ladies' night, but then realized I didn't have anywhere to go but here, so here I am. I'll need to stay for a bit, if that's okay with you."

"You know you're always welcome here," she tells me. "It's only ever been the two of us, Ash. The only person I can always count on is you."

Her words bring tears to my eyes and I blink rapidly to keep them from rolling down my cheeks.

"Yeah, at least we have each other." I lean back in the chair and blow out a breath, wondering where in the hell my life went so wrong. I'm twenty-five and a college dropout. I can't even keep a steady waitressing job—or a boyfriend, apparently, that either doesn't think he can put his hands on me or cheat on me. I guess the statistics aren't in my favor, seeing as I'm falling right into my mom's steps and following in her example.

"I'm going to head off to bed," I say a few minutes later. "I love you, Mom."

I head down the hall to my old room, the one I've come and gone from over the years. This isn't the first time I've had to move back home with my mom, but god, do I wish it could be the last. I toss my purse and cell on the bed, then head into the bathroom. Thankfully, I'm able to rummage through the cabinet and find a new toothbrush; one of the free ones the dentist gives you at an appointment. After finishing up in the bathroom, I head back into the bedroom and rummage through the dresser, finding an old t-shirt and some shorts to sleep in. In my haste to get out of my apartment earlier, I didn't grab anything but what I already had on me when I walked in and then right back out.

I pull back the covers and slip between the cool sheets. This bed is anything but comfortable, but it's better than sleeping in my car. I remember the day my mom found it on Craigslist for free. I'd been sleeping on the couch for a few months by that point, and desperately needed a bed of my own. It was already old and lumpy when she got it all those years ago, but we've always lived paycheck to paycheck, and replacing it was never in the budget.

I was lucky to have enough clothes to get me through the week, and to have food in the house some days. There were a few times the only meal I ate each day was the free lunch from school, and or the food my friends would insist I take from them. I always did my best to hide what my home life was like; it was embarrassing to admit it to my friends my mom was poor. It also didn't help she didn't make the best decisions when it came to men coming in and out of our life.

I stare up at the ceiling, willing the tears not to start flowing once again. I make a promise to myself, tomorrow will be a new day. I'll hit the ground running, finding as many places as I can to fill out applications, to get a new job as soon as possible. I should have asked Nick if they were hiring for any servers. It seemed like a pretty busy place, so maybe I can stop back there tomorrow and see about a job. At this point, I don't really care what the job is. As long as it's not stripping, and pays me, I'm happy.

I check my cell one last time, realizing I don't have a charger for it. Thankfully, it was still charged to about fifty percent, so I put it into airplane mode for the night before finally falling to sleep.

I WAKE BY EIGHT THE NEXT MORNING, STRETCHING as soon as I wake up from the lumpy mattress. I drag myself out of bed and into the kitchen to make a pot of coffee to help wake myself up. As I wait for the coffee to brew, I lean against the kitchen counter and stare out the window.

"You're up early." My mom's raspy voice startles me out of my daydream.

"Yeah," I say, pulling a cup out of the cabinet and filling it up with the hot coffee, then adding a little bit of milk. I take the first drink, savoring the taste and warmth of it. "I'm going to hit the ground running, so to speak, today. Apply for any and all jobs I can find and go get my stuff from the apartment. I didn't bring anything with me yesterday. Do you think you could give me a ride over to my car this morning?"

"Sure, let me take a shower and we can leave."

"Thanks, Mom," I tell her before she disappears around the corner and into the bathroom. I hear the shower turn on and I settle in at the small two-person kitchen table to finish my coffee and eat a bagel from the bag on the counter.

I finish my quick breakfast and make my way back into my room, where I change into a pair of shorts I found in the drawer last night and my top from yester-day. My first stop will be my old apartment to pack up my things, and then I'll start driving around to places to find a new job.

"Ready?" my mom says, sticking her head into the doorway.

"Yep," I say, jumping up and sliding my shoes on. I grab my purse and sling it over my shoulder as I follow her out to her car.

"Where am I dropping you off at?" she asks, buckling her seat belt before backing out of the parking spot.

"Tiffany's place." Tiffany is my best friend, who I went out with last night. I drove to her place after I left Chris and my apartment, and she ended up driving us to the bar.

"How is she doing?" Mom asks as she turns out onto the main road.

"Good, the wedding is quickly approaching."

"About damn time they get married," Mom comments.

"She wasn't in any rush," I say on a laugh. Tiffany has been my best friend since elementary school, and one of the only people in this world who knows just how shitty a childhood I had. She knows all my deepest secrets and fears. She's my ride-or-die, the sister I never had. I'd be lost or dead if it wasn't for her. And she's finally marrying her high school sweetheart, Colton, this summer.

We pull into her driveway and Mom drops me off. "Thanks for the ride, I'll see you later."

"I'm working tonight, so I'll be home late," she tells me.

"Then I'll see you when I see you." I give her a smile before I shut the car door, then walk over to my car. I'm not even going to bother knocking, since both Tiffany and Colton are at work right now.

I start my car and immediately plug my cell into the cigarette lighter charger. By keeping it in airplane mode last night, that helped save my battery overnight, but I'm going to need it later when I start applying for jobs. I turn on my service and ignore the incoming texts. I only have one thing on my mind right now.

Ashley: I'm headed to the apartment to get my things, please don't be there when I arrive. I won't touch your shit, so you don't have to worry about that. I'll also be stopping by the leasing office and taking my name off the lease. Don't fight me on it. If you get called by them to verify you're okay with this, I expect you to agree to it. It's the least you can do after fucking that chick in our apartment.

With my text to Chris sent, I pull out of Tiffany's place and drive the few miles over to my old apartment. Thankfully, when I pull in, I don't see his car in the parking lot. He should be at work at this time of day, but I obviously don't know his schedule as well as I thought I did.

I head inside and go straight for the kitchen cabinet, pulling out a few trash bags. I mostly just have clothes and toiletries to pack up, so trash bags it is.

I make quick work of packing up my clothes and then head into the bathroom. Since I want to get out and apply for jobs as soon as possible, I jump in the shower and change into some black pants and a nice top. I actually take the time to blow dry and style my hair, rather than pull it back into my normal ponytail. After applying a little makeup—just a bit of mascara, concealer, and some lip gloss—I toss the remaining things into one last bag and then start hauling them to my car. All the furniture belonged to Chris, or things we bought cheap from thrift stores over the last few months we lived together.

I head for the mall, knowing a large number of stores and restaurants are located in that area. As much as I'd love to go back to school and finish my degree, I just can't afford to do that right now. It's been my dream to become a counselor and work with women and kids, but I don't see that happening anytime soon.

A few hours later, I've accomplished what I set out to do and applied for as many jobs as I possibly could. I saw a sign while I was in the mall, advertising a temp agency, so I snapped a picture of their information and plan to look at their website, so I can sign up with them to be considered for jobs they are tasked to fill.

Hopefully, something will pan out, sooner rather than later.

3

NICK

"Hey, bro," Kaiden calls out to me when I walk into the office above the bar.

"Mornin'." I take a pull from the to-go cup of coffee in my hand. "Ready to take inventory?" I ask him as I drop into the seat across the desk from him. His eyes are glued to the computer screen as he looks over the numbers from the last couple of days.

"Things are up this week," he tells me, looking away from the screen.

"That's great. I've definitely noticed an uptick in customers lately. Our new marketing campaign must be working well."

"It sure is. I've tweaked some of the ads just a little bit over the weeks, and think we've finally got one converting really well. Offering up that coupon was a genius idea," Kaiden tells me.

Kaiden hands me a clipboard with column after

column of inventory items. "Shall we?" he says, standing up and heading downstairs into our stockroom. When we first renovated, we made sure it had plenty of space and was well-organized. It takes us about two hours to inventory everything between the stockroom and the kitchen, then to get our order in for the week.

After opening, there was a learning curve for a few months before we got a good system down on how to order correctly, so we didn't over or under order, especially when it came to the food aspect of the bar. Liquor and beer last a little longer than food items do, but once we got in a groove, things started running a whole lot easier.

"Have you given any more thought to hiring another bartender?" I ask Kaiden, once we've submitted the orders to our distributors.

"I have, and after running the numbers, I think we can finally afford one. It'll be nice to have one more on staff and will allow the two of us to take an extra night off each week, which I think we've both earned."

"That sure will be nice," I agree. Working six to seven days a week for the last five years has been stressful at times. If either one of us wants to take time off, the other is left to cover.

"If you're good with it, I'll get something posted stating we're hiring, and start the process. Hopefully, we'll be able to do some interviews as early as next week and get someone in here within the next couple of weeks for training."

"Sounds good to me. Just let me know when you set up the interviews and I'll make sure to clear my schedule."

I head back downstairs to the bar to start our opening procedures. We don't open up for another two hours, but that time will fly by before we know it. Before I start pulling down chairs, I head into the kitchen and find one of our cooks, Ryan.

"Hey, man," he greets as I walk through the swinging doors.

"Hey, Ryan, can I get a cheeseburger and fries?" I ask, after bumping his fist with my own.

"Sure can, I'll bring it out once it's ready. I've got to turn on the fryer still, so give me a little bit."

"Thanks, I'll be getting things ready for opening," I tell him before heading back out into the bar area. I start by taking all the chairs down that have been up on the tables, then make my way behind the bar to look over what all needs to be restocked for the night ahead of us. With it being Friday night, we'll be pretty busy all night long.

"One cheeseburger with fries," Ryan says, setting the plate down on the bar in front of me.

My stomach picks that moment to grumble really loud, pulling a laugh from my lips. "Thanks, guess I was hungry," I tell him before I take a huge bite of the burger. The flavor hits my tongue and I about melt in my spot. Ryan is a fantastic cook; one we are damn lucky to have on our staff. "I didn't know a burger could taste so amazing," I add, by way of a compliment.

"Glad you approve," he says on a laugh as he turns and walks back to his domain in the kitchen. I quickly scarf down my food, then place the plate in a bussing tub under the bar, and get back to my opening tasks. Once the ice bins are both full and I've got all the garnish tubs filled, I switch to stocking the liquor bottles, pulling out new ones for the bottles that are almost empty and that we tend to go through each night.

With it being Friday night, we typically get busy early and stay that way until closing time on the weekends.

"Hey, Nick," Katie greets me as she comes in the back door. "Need any help getting things ready?"

"Hey," I say, waving from across the bar. "I've got everything done, for the most part. Feel free to head on upstairs and see Kaiden if you'd like. I'll get the doors opened here in a little bit."

"Sounds good. Sorry I wasn't here earlier. My appointment was late getting started as my doctor was running late," she tells me.

"Everything okay?" I ask, concern lacing my voice.

"Oh, yeah. Just my annual exam. My doc got called out to a delivery at the hospital, so her afternoon appointments were just pushed back."

"Ah, gotcha." I wipe the bar top down one last time before it's opening time.

"I'll be right back. Holler if you need me sooner," she says, taking the stairs two at a time up to the office, where Kaiden is probably still sitting doing paperwork.

Since the day we decided to open this business together, we've split as many of the tasks as we can down the middle. He's better at the computer and money shit and I'm better at the actual bar-related things. He keeps the money coming and I keep the booze flowing. While he does get behind the bar plenty, and knows how to make anything a customer orders, if he could choose between being behind the bar versus the computer crunching numbers, paying the bills, or ordering supplies, he'd choose the latter first every time.

I head over and flip the open sign and unlock the doors, then head back behind the bar to wait for the first rush of customers. We open at four p.m. during the week and at noon on the weekends, to take advantage of the customers looking to grab a burger and beer, and watch their favorite sports team playing on one of our many TV screens.

THE FIRST WAVE OF CUSTOMERS STARTED ROLLING in shortly after we open and don't stop coming in until well after midnight. Before I know it, I'm ringing the bell, calling out last call for the night. I'm exhausted by the time I'm ready to leave at almost three a.m.

I make it home and head straight for my bedroom, stripping out of my clothes and taking a quick shower to wash the stench of alcohol, sweat, and bar food from my skin. Thankfully, we have an opening crew that will be in tomorrow to open the bar up. I'm not due to show up until six tomorrow night, to work the closing shift all over again.

I dry off and slip on a pair of boxer briefs, then head out to my kitchen to grab a glass of water and flip through my mail that came today. Nothing but junk and a few bills that are all automatically paid, so nothing I have to worry about. I'm dead on my feet, so once I finish my glass of water, I set the glass on the counter and head back into my room, crashing hard as soon as my head hits the pillow.

4

ASHLEY

"Hey, Mom."

"How was your night?" she asks, finally waking up after her late night at work.

"Good, just stayed home and got all my things unpacked and put away. How was work?"

"Busy. Lots of calls last night," she says as she pours a cup of coffee. She's been a dispatcher for almost twenty years now, and has worked the third shift for the last eight or so.

"Helps the night go by fast," I muse, drinking my second cup of coffee.

"Sure does," she confirms. "Got any plans for today?"

"Yeah," I say, blowing out a breath. "Tiff's birthday is Monday, so we're celebrating tonight."

"What are you girls doing to celebrate?"

"Dinner and hitting up a few bars is the last thing I heard. We've got a big group going."

"Sounds like fun, be safe."

"Always," I state. "Do you work tonight?"

"Yep, next three nights." She takes a seat on the couch and props her feet up on the coffee table. "Any luck with the job search yesterday?"

"Hopefully. I applied at a handful of places around and in the mall. Right now, I'd be happy with pretty much any job. I was also going to apply with a temp agency that had an advertisement at the mall," I tell her, remembering I snapped a picture of their sign. "I need to look at their website from a computer, so had to wait to do so until I was home, and I forgot about it."

I grab my laptop from the end table next to me. It takes it a good five minutes to fully load since it's so old and slow, but it still works for the few things I need a computer for, so I'm in no rush to replace it.

"An office job with normal hours would be nice," she says.

"Maybe. I'm so used to working evenings and serving that I'm not sure I'll like an office job long-term, but like I said earlier, I just need a job. I can't afford not to have an income coming in."

"I'm sure something will come along next week."

"I sure hope so." I know I've got a little cushion in my account, but I'd rather not drain my savings account down to nothing. So, after tonight, no more going out until I'm back on my feet. No unnecessary spending, no stops at Starbucks or fast food. Tonight is my last hurrah until I can land a job and have a few paychecks under my belt.

"Happy birthday!" I call out as I walk into Tiffany and Colton's house.

"Thank you!" Tiffany squeals from the top of the stairs.

"Are you ready for tonight?" I ask as I climb the stairs and then wrap her in a hug.

"Sure am!" she exclaims. "Are you ready?"

"I was born ready," I joke.

"We're going to have so much fun!" The doorbell rings and she yells, "Come in!"

In walk three girls I've only met once before, who all work with Tiffany. "Hey, girls!" Tiffany exclaims when she sees who has arrived. "I know y'all have met once before, but just in case you don't remember, Ashley, this is Holly, Nikki, and Zara. Ladies, this is my best friend, my ride-or-die, Ashley."

"Nice to see y'all again," I say as they come up the stairs.

"You too," they all chime in, smiling.

"I've got some snacks and shots ready for us in the kitchen. Figured we could get the party started before we even leave the house," Tiffany tells everyone.

"Sounds good to me," Holly says as we all make our way into the kitchen.

Nikki picks up a Jell-O shot. "These look awesome."

"I love me some Jell-O shots, so figured I'd make us up some to pre-party with."

"Is anyone else coming tonight?" Zara asks.

"Not for the entire night. My sister-in-law, Danielle, is going to meet us at the restaurant for dinner and maybe hit up one bar. It all just depends on what time it is when we're finished with dinner."

"If we're ready to head toward dinner, I can get our Uber ordered and on its way," I offer, pulling my phone out a little while later. The Jell-O shots are starting to take effect, and I'm feeling a nice buzz beginning.

"I'm ready," Tiffany states. "You girls ready?"

"We're ready," they all confirm, and I get the Uber app pulled up and our ride ordered.

"We've got about ten minutes before our car arrives, so down another shot, use the ladies' room, and let's get this party on the road." I pick up a shot glass and hold it up for everyone to do the same. "A quick toast before we really get this party started. Happy birthday, Tiffany. May your twenty-sixth year be the most amazing year you've ever had! Cheers, ladies."

"Cheers!" everyone exclaims, as we all clink glasses before downing our shots.

Dinner passes by in a blur of great food and even

better conversation. We had dinner at Tiffany's favorite place, a sushi and teppanyaki restaurant. The food was fantastic, as it always is here.

"Shall we head to the first bar on our stop?" Nikki asks, as we all finish up paying our bills with the waitress.

"Sounds good to me," Tiffany confirms.

"Good, because I've got the Uber ordered, and the driver will be here in just a couple of minutes," Nikki tells us, so we head up to the front doors and wait outside for the guy to pull up.

"The first stop on our tour is Tootsie's!" Nikki announces as we drive down the highway.

"Yes!" Tiffany calls out. The stops planned for tonight have been kept a secret from the birthday girl. Each of us picked a place to stop at for a little while tonight while we celebrate her birthday.

With our first round of drinks in our cover charge-stamped hands, we head for the dance floor. With it being Saturday night, the stage is filled with a band hoping to make it in the country music industry. They're pretty good, singing mostly covers and a few original songs during their set.

"You ladies ready to hit our next stop?" Tiffany asks, once there's a lull in the music as the bands switch out.

"We're ready!" we all answer at the same time.

"Next stop is Second Fiddle," Zara calls out.

We leave Tootsie's and head next door to Second

Fiddle. With another set of hand stamps and drinks, our time at Second Fiddle, then at Holly's pick, all go the same. Drinks, dancing, and celebrating our girl. At each bar, we fend off different groups of guys, who all buy us rounds of drinks and attempt to dance with us, hoping to score and take someone home with them tonight. Little do they all realize, out of the five of us, I'm the only single one in the group.

"All right, ladies, we've got one last stop," I tell them, a little after midnight. "We're headed to The Tap House for one last round of drinks and some of the best greasy bar food around."

"I love it there!" Tiffany slurs slightly.

"I've got the Uber ordered, so hit up the bathroom and let's meet outside."

Tiffany, Nikki, and I head for the doors to wait outside while Holly and Zara stop by the bathroom. Thankfully, the lines must be short as they find us outside just as our ride pulls up.

"Evening, ladies," our driver greets us as we all pile in his minivan.

"Good evening."

"I've got The Tap House as a destination, is that correct?" he asks, before pulling away from the curb.

"That's correct," I confirm.

"Perfect. You ladies having a good night?"

"We sure are," Tiffany tells him. "My girls, here, sure do know how to celebrate a birthday."

"Well, happy birthday," he says on a laugh.

With the late hour, we make it the few miles to The Tap House fairly quickly. "Thanks for the ride," I tell him as we all exit the van. I look around to make sure no one left anything, and see Tiffany's phone sitting on the seat.

"Hey, Tiff," I call out as she stands a few feet away from me on the curb. "You forgetting something?" I tease, as I hand her the phone.

"Thank you!" she squeals. "That would have totally sucked to lose my phone tonight."

"Yes, it would," I agree as we make our way inside. I quickly scan the place, looking for a table for us to occupy, so we can order some food to help soak up the alcohol we've consumed tonight. I see one fairly close to the bar and make a beeline for it.

"The nachos are amazing. I had some the other night when I was here," I tell the girls as we all gather round the table.

"Yes! We need an order of those, along with the giant pretzel with beer cheese," Tiffany says.

"That sounds good to me," Holly states as a waitress approaches the table.

"Evening, ladies," she says, setting down a round of shot glasses.

"We didn't order those," Zara tells her.

"Oh, I'm aware," she says, a huge smile on her face. "These are on the house, sent straight from the bartender himself." She motions over her shoulder to the guy behind the bar. I look over and notice it's Nick, the same guy from the other night who saved me and was so, so kind to me.

"Thank you!" Tiffany yells, lifting her shot glass up and nodding her head to Nick.

He laughs at her drunkenness and mouths back, "You're welcome," before he turns his attention to the full bar in front of him.

We place our order for both food and drinks, then sit back to relax for a little bit. We've been on our feet almost all night, and I know my feet are killing me, so the break from dancing is much needed.

"Thank you, girls, for the incredible night. I know it isn't over yet, but I wanted to tell you all that before we parted ways. I love you all so much and am so blessed to have you all in my life."

"Aww, we love you, too," we tell her at the same time, sending us all into a fit of giggles.

"Ladies." A deep rumbling voice from behind me sends a hush over our table, and I immediately know who it is. "I've got an order of nachos and a giant pretzel with extra beer cheese," Nick says, as he sets the two plates down on the table, along with some small plates for each of us to use. "Can I get anyone anything else?"

"We're good," we state as we dig in to the food in front of us.

"All right." He laughs as he watches us all stuff our faces with huge bites of food. "If that changes, just flag one of us down," he says before retreating from our table to back behind the bar.

"Ready to dance?" Tiffany asks everyone, once we've finished all the food and drained our drinks.

"Maybe for a few more minutes," Holly says. "After eating and sitting for a while, I'm starting to feel tired. It's past my bedtime." She laughs, and Zara and Nikki agree with her.

"We can head out if you guys want to go," I offer.

"No, we'd hate to make you guys leave before you're ready. We can always grab our own Ubers home. I was just going to leave my car at Tiff's until tomorrow anyways," Holly states.

"If you're sure?" Tiffany says to them.

"Of course. You stay and enjoy your night out," they tell her.

Tiffany and I make our way over to the dance floor as the other girls head out for the night. We dance the next hour or so away and before we know it, Nick is ringing a bell and calling out for last call. We make our way over to the bar and each order one last drink, as well as a glass of water.

"You ladies have a fun night?" he asks as he shakes up our drinks.

"The best!" Tiffany tells him over the loud music.

"What are y'all out celebrating?" he asks, pointing to all the stamps on our hands.

"This one's birthday," I tell him, wrapping an arm around Tiffany's shoulder.

"Well, happy birthday." He pushes our glasses across the bar in front of us. I hold up my debit card for him to take and he shakes his head at me. "These are on the house. A birthday gift, of sorts," he says as I try and protest.

"Thank you!" Tiffany takes a drink. "This is so good," she tells him as he pours a beer from the tap in front of us.

"I'm glad you like it," he says as he hands off the glass of beer.

We bring our drinks back to the table we occupied earlier. The crowd has definitely thinned out since we got here earlier, but there's still a decent group of people finishing up their last drink of the night.

"Are we splitting an Uber back to my place, or what's the plan?" Tiffany asks once we've finished our drinks.

"I knew I wouldn't be able to drive tonight, so I just took an Uber to your place. I can just grab my own, since we're going in opposite directions from here."

"Now that you mention it, I realized your car wasn't in my driveway when we left for dinner."

"Figured that was the best option," I tell her as I finish off my glass of water. "I'm going to stick around for a few minutes and talk to Nick."

"Yeah, what's up with that?" she asks, eyeing him behind the bar.

"Nothing's up with that. He saved me the other

night after you left, that's all. Took pity on the girl that was crying in one of his booths."

"And tonight... the free shots, free drinks?" she states.

"That, I have no clue about. I didn't even realize he was here until the shots were delivered and the server said they were from him."

"I think someone likes you," she says in a teasing voice.

"Shut up." I smack at her shoulder. "And it doesn't matter anyways. I've sworn off men. They're all bad news. Well, except Colton."

"Ashley, you'll find a good one, just give it time. I promise you, they're not all toads. You'll find your Prince Charming one of these days."

"If you say so," I tell her, blowing out a huge breath.

5

NICK

I WIPE DOWN THE BAR AGAIN AS I WATCH ASHLEY and her friend in my peripheral vision. I noticed her group as soon as she walked in tonight. I tend to watch the door as each customer comes and goes; just something I've always done since we opened. It helps me keep tabs on what's going on in the bar, especially when it's busy like it is tonight. Her group looked like they were having a great time tonight, laughing constantly as they sat around, eating and drinking.

With last call over, and the crowd dispersing as everyone finishes up their last drinks of the night, I watch as the one last friend that was with Ashley heads out the door before she does.

"Need another water or soda?" I call out to her from behind the bar.

"Another water would be great," she tells me, moving over to sit on a bar stool in front of me.

"What happened to your group?" I ask, placing the glass of ice water in front of her.

"Some left earlier, as they were tired. Tiffany just went home in an Uber. I need to get one, as well."

"Why didn't you go together?" I ask curiously.

"We live in opposite directions, so it made more sense to take separate ones," she says, taking a drink of her water. "Thanks again for the free shots and drinks tonight."

"You're welcome. Looked like you ladies enjoyed yourselves." I place all my shaker cups in the dish tub as I start my cleanup process. "How'd everything turn out after the other night?" I ask curiously.

"Nothing really to turn out. I applied for a bunch of jobs yesterday, after I moved all my things out of my apartment with my ex and into my mom's place. Thankfully, she was willing to let me move back in. Not exactly where I thought I'd be living at this point in my life, but I also didn't quite expect to be jobless, either. Shit, sorry, I'm rambling again," she says, clamping her lips together to keep from saying anything else.

I don't know what it is about her, but she's cute when she's flustered like this.

"Well, I hope things turn around for you soon. I'm sure a job will come through for you before long."

"Hopefully," she says, blowing out a big breath, one strong enough to flutter the hairs framing her face.

"If you want to hang around until I'm done, I can

give you a ride home," I find myself offering. "Save yourself the Uber fare."

"That's okay, I wouldn't want to be a bother."

"Not a bother. I'm the one that offered, after all."

"Okay then," she says, biting her bottom lip, and I find my dick rising to attention at that.

"It will take me a half hour, forty-five minutes, tops, to finish up my closing procedures. Would you like anything before I get to work?"

"I'm good. Thanks, Nick," she says, smiling at me. "If anything, can I help do something so you can get out of here sooner?"

"We're fine. Just pick a booth and sit back and relax. We've got a good routine," I tell her as Katie and Kaiden both start flipping chairs up on the tables before we mop the floors.

I focus on cleaning the bar and restocking a few bottles I used up tonight. Once I have the bar all cleaned and ready for tomorrow's opening crew, I check in with Kaiden, who's already balanced our tills out for the night and dropped the cash into the safe we keep in the office until he can prepare the deposits after the weekend.

"Good night tonight," Kaiden says, slapping me on the shoulder.

"It sure was. Steady all night."

"It was fun being behind the bar with you tonight."

"Yeah, it was," I agree. We usually only end up

behind the bar together on our busiest nights—Thursday through Saturday.

"What's up with the chick?" he asks, motioning his head in Ashley's direction. "You don't usually take someone home with you at the end of a shift."

"Just giving her a ride home. We met the other night and she's had a bad week. Just trying to do something friendly," I tell him honestly.

"So, you're not tapping that?" he asks, a shit-eating grin on his face.

"Nope," I tell him, popping the P. "At least not tonight. She's had way too much to drink to make that decision clearly tonight."

"So, what I'm hearing is that you wouldn't mind tapping that," he asks, still boasting the shit-eating grin.

"I wouldn't turn it down if offered under the right conditions, and her three sheets to the wind isn't the right conditions," I deadpan.

"I hear ya," he says, looking around for Katie. "Been there, done that, brother." He smacks my shoulder. "I'm off to find my wife and take her home. See you tomorrow."

He walks off in search for his wife and I approach the booth where Ashley is sitting. "You ready?"

"Yeah," she says sleepily, then yawns. "I almost fell asleep."

"Well, then let's get you home." I hold my hand out for her. She accepts it and slides out of the booth, and keeping her hand wrapped in mine, I lead her through the bar and out the back door. I lock it up quickly and then escort her to my truck parked just a few feet from the back entrance.

"Where to?" I ask, once buckled in the driver's seat. A few minutes later, with the address to her mom's place programmed into my GPS, I pull out of the parking lot and onto the main street.

"Where all did you apply for jobs?" I break the silence filling my truck.

"A bunch of places in the mall and surrounding buildings. I don't really care what I get a job doing, as long as they pay and it's full-time, I'll take it. I just need anything, at this point. I can get picky later, once I have a good job under my belt, and steady income."

"Have you ever tended bar?" I ask, knowing we're going to be hiring a new bartender soon.

"Nope, I've usually worked at diners that either didn't have a liquor license, or only served beer and wine. Why do you ask?"

"We might be hiring for a new bartender. Thought I'd tell you about the opening, if you'd be interested in it."

"Oh, thanks for thinking of me. I'm not sure I'd be good for the position, not having ever tended bar before. Especially with how busy you guys stay most nights."

"You'd be surprised how quickly you pick up mixing all the drinks," I tell her as I drive down the street. "That, and we fully train our bartenders, and have new ones work the easier shifts to start out. We wouldn't throw you to the wolves," I add on a laugh.

"Maybe. I'll keep the option open and see what comes of all the applications I put in today."

"Sounds good," I tell her as I quickly look over at her and take in her relaxed state. She's got her head resting on the headrest, and her eyes are closed from what I can tell by my quick look at her.

I continue driving, following the GPS directions as we fall into a silence. I'm not one hundred percent sure, but I think Ashley might have fallen asleep in the passenger seat. My suspicions are confirmed when I pull into the lot of the apartment building and park.

"Ash," I say, somewhat quietly as I run the backs of my fingers down her cheek. "We're at your place."

Her eyes pop open and she looks around, then straight at me, a little shocked at her surroundings.

"Crap, sorry for falling asleep," she says, sitting up and rubbing her eyes.

"It's okay," I reassure her. "It's late, and from the sounds of it, you had a busy night."

She yawns. "Yeah."

"I'll walk you in, make sure you make it inside okay." I get out and walk around to open her door, then offer her my hand to steady herself as she stands up. I slip it around her, resting my hand on her hip as I pull her against my side as we walk into the building. "What unit?" I ask, once inside the hallway.

"Number two," she says, motioning down the hall.

We walk back to the door marked with a metal number two. Ashley pulls out her keys and unlocks the door, opening it to a dark apartment. "Would you like to come in?" she asks, looking up at me with a mixture of drunkenness and desire in her eyes.

"I'll come in to make sure you get settled tonight, but for nothing else." She pushes her bottom lip out in a pout and it's just about the fucking cutest thing I've ever seen. "Sorry, darlin', but you've had too much to drink tonight to make any decisions like that," I tell her as I nudge her to move inside.

She reaches in and flips a switch that turns on a lamp in the living room. The unit isn't huge, but it's homey.

"Let's get you in and into bed." I follow her back to her room, standing at the doorway as she rummages through her drawers, pulling out a tank top and shorts. I step aside so she can exit her room and head into the bathroom. While she's in there, I lean back against the wall, looking up at the ceiling, and blow out a big breath. *What the fuck am I doing here?* I see her phone laying on the bed and her charger on the nightstand, so I grab it, plugging it in so she doesn't forget or lose it in her sheets overnight and end up with a dead battery in the morning.

The bathroom door opening draws my attention, and I look over just as Ashley is coming out. She's pulled her hair up into a messy bun that's sitting on top of her head, and the tank top is tight and leaves little to the imagination. I can easily see her hardened nipples and the outline of her areoles. The sight of her curvy body in the tiny shorts and tight tank top has my dick pressing against the zipper of my jeans.

She closes the space between the bathroom door and where I'm standing at her bedroom door, stopping in front of me. She looks up at me, that drunk lust still filling her eyes. "Are you sure I can't change your mind about staying?" she asks then nibbles on her bottom lip and fuck if my dick doesn't twitch and harden a little more in my jeans.

"I meant what I said earlier. You're in no condition to make those kinds of decisions right now. Maybe another time, Ash, when you haven't had so much to drink and can make that decision with a clear mind." I will not budge from my stance on this. I would never push myself on a girl, and don't want one regretting a decision made when drunk come the next morning.

"You're one of a kind," she whispers between us, then turns and walks into her room. She tosses her clothes into a hamper in the corner before she lies down.

I walk back out to the living room to leave and notice her keys are still in the lock, so I take them out and place them on kitchen counter, where she's sure to find them. I find a sticky note pad on the counter and scribble out my cell number and leave it stuck to her keys.

"I took your keys from the lock, I left them on the

counter. Call or text me in the morning, tell me if you're okay. Also take these, and drink this," I tell her, handing her a couple ibuprofen I found in a bottle on the counter, along with a glass of water. She does as I tell her and then collapses on the pillow. I look over her one last time, pretty sure she won't remember much of this conversation, then leave her bedroom.

I shut the door behind me but leave on the lamp and turn the lock on the handle of the door since I can't lock the deadbolt without the keys. I left her alone, to sleep off the alcohol. Hopefully, she'll call or text me in the morning.

6

ASHLEY

I WAKE UP AND LOOK AROUND AT MY ROOM. I vaguely remember coming home with Nick last night, after being out for Tiffany's birthday party and ending the night at The Tap House. I roll over onto my back and realize the other side of my bed is empty and cold, so Nick either never slept there or has already left. After pulling the blankets off and realizing I'm in my normal sleep clothes, I'm going to guess he didn't stay, and we didn't sleep together. How pathetic must I be that I can't remember exactly what happened last night?

After using the bathroom, I wash my hands and face, then brush my teeth. Once I feel human again, I make my way out to the kitchen. Mom's door is shut, which doesn't surprise me, since she worked a night shift and it's only ten. I notice my keys sitting on the counter with a sticky note attached to them, so I grab it after starting the coffee pot.

Ash – you left these in the lock last night, not sure where you normally keep them, but figured here was better than in the lock. Call or text me when you wake up, so I know you're okay. – Nick

I read his note a few more times, wondering what kind of man does this. What kind of man drives a drunk girl home and makes sure she gets to bed safely? What sort of man picks up my life I've practically thrown on the floor, left my keys he found in my door and his number on the counter, and then walked out? Who doesn't take advantage of the drunk girl who throws herself at him, offering up her body? Maybe he's got a girlfriend? Maybe he swings for the other team? No way. I saw the way he looked at me, how I affected him. How he held my hand last night leaving the bar. He's definitely attracted.

I sit with a mug of coffee, fingering the sticky note with Nick's note and cell number on it. I ponder if I should contact him. He was super nice to do every-thing he did for me last night, so it would be rude *not* to at least text him, to let him know I'm okay and to thank him for getting me home safe last night.

With two cups of coffee consumed and a small breakfast of some buttered toast, I make my way back into my room and grab my cell from my nightstand. It was plugged in, so at least it isn't dead somewhere—probably another thing Nick did for me last night. I quickly add his contact information into my phone and then open my messaging app.

> Hey, thanks for the ride home last night and for making sure I made it inside and to bed safely. You're one of a kind, Nick.

I don't really expect to hear back from him, especially this early in the day with the hours he works at the bar, so I toss my phone back onto my nightstand and slide back under the covers. I don't have any real plans today, so a little more sleep sounds about perfect right now.

I WAKE UP A WHILE LATER, FEELING REFRESHED. I grab my cell to check the time and am shocked I slept for another three hours. I also have a couple missed texts from Nick and Tiffany.

TIFFANY

> Are you alive? Did you make it home safely? Anything fun happen with the sexy bartender?

Ash… text me, call me… I just want to make sure you're okay. Fuck, I should have never left you at that bar last night.

I really hope you're just asleep and not dead in some alley somewhere.

NICK

Really it wasn't a big deal. I'm glad I was able to get you home safely. Since you found my note with my number, I take it you also found your keys.

Want to grab a late lunch? I can come pick you up.

Crap, I hate it when Tiffany worries about me, so I answer her first.

Sorry! I'm safe at home. Nick got me home last night, nothing fun happened. He was a complete gentleman. But he did text me, asking if I wanted to go grab a late lunch with him… Tell me what to do!?!?

Yes! I found my keys. Thank you for removing them from the lock. I can't believe I left them in it. :head desk:

TIFFANY

Girl, you had me freaking out. I was about to head down to The Tap House and start questioning the workers to find out when you left last night. So, I'm glad to hear you're alive.

So, he took you home, huh?

Yes. He offered to drive me home to save me the cost of an Uber. I stuck around the bar while he closed down and then he drove me home. I ended up falling asleep on the way home, so he helped get me inside. I was a mess, Tiff. Like, drunk girl, life's in complete disarray, huge fucking mess. I vaguely remember inviting him to stay, but him kindly turning me down. Said I'd had too much to drink to make a decision like that. But I know he was attracted to me. He left a note with his cell number and my keys—which I'd apparently left in the door when we got here—on the counter. I texted him earlier when I woke up for a little bit, thanking him for the ride and apologizing for my hot mess express of a life. So, I was a little shocked at the lunch invite.

TIFFANY

There is so much to unpack from all of that. Please tell me you said yes to the lunch invite. Any guy who would tell you you've had too much to drink to make the decision to sleep together is one you pursue. He sounds like a good guy, Ash.

I'm sure he's a great guy, but I just got out of a relationship. Should I really be jumping right back into the dating pool?

NICK

No worries. We've all had nights like that. I've done some stupid shit a time or two while drunk. Don't worry, I won't hold it against you. ;)

Did you want to grab lunch? I was about to head out to grab something… I can swing by and pick you up if you want.

He's texting me again asking about lunch—tell me what to do!!!

TIFFANY

Tell him yes!

Are you sure? I haven't even showered yet and he said he's ready to leave his house.

TIFFANY

Yes, I'm sure. Now get your ass into the shower. You've got a sexy bartender to impress. I expect details later!

Okay, you've convinced me.

Lunch sounds great, but I haven't showered yet. Can you stall for twenty, maybe twenty-five minutes?

NICK

Sure can. I'll see you soon.

It's a done deal. I told him yes! I'm off to shower as I told him it would only take me twenty minutes to be ready.

TIFFANY

I want details later. You better not
forget to call me.

I'll think about it. ;)

I pull up my latest audiobook and turn on my shower speaker. With the words and sexy timbre of one of my favorite narrators filling the bathroom, I take one of the fastest showers I can, yet still taking the time to run a razor over all the necessary places.

After drying off, I head into my room, closing the door behind me and opening the closet. I stand in front of it, my towel wrapped around my body, as I stare at my options. I have no idea what to wear for this lunch date.

I grab a sundress but put it back. I pull out a tank top and some shorts and toss them over to my bed as an option, then pull out a pair of capris and another tank top, tossing it to join the pile on my bed. I snag a bra and one of my favorite pairs of panties from my bin in the closet and start getting dressed.

Standing in front of my closed door that has a full-length mirror hanging off the back, I hold up the first option in front of me, then swap it for the other option as I compare the two.

I finally settle on the shorts, but with the second tank top. Shows off just enough skin and cleavage, but not too much to be inappropriate.

With my outfit settled on, I head back into the

bathroom and brush my hair, then quickly braid it to keep it out of my face. After brushing my teeth, I swipe on some mascara and lip gloss and check myself over in the mirror. Approving of my look, I head back into my room and slip on some cute sandals, then grab my purse just as I hear a knock on the door.

"Hey!" I greet Nick as I open the door. My eyes rake over his body, taking in his casual look of a tighter t-shirt and some jeans.

"Hey, yourself," he says, as he looks me up and down, then notices my purse. "You ready?"

"Yep, perfect timing. I just finished getting ready."

"Then, let's get out of here, I'm starving."

"I wouldn't want to keep you waiting then," I joke as we walk out the door. I stop briefly to lock up, before Nick escorts me down the hall and out the door.

"Any requests or suggestions on where to go for lunch?" he asks as he opens his truck door for me and offers a hand for me to climb up.

"Nope, I'm pretty open," I tell him before he closes the door. I click my seat belt into place while I watch him round the front and then climb in himself.

"Do you like wings and beer?" he asks as he backs out of the parking spot.

"Isn't it un-American to *not* like wings and beer?" I ask jokingly.

"Sure is." He chuckles from the driver seat. "I'm about to blow your socks off then. This place might be the smallest dive restaurant in the city, but damn, do they have the best wings known to man."

"Sounds perfect, just no judging me if I use my fingers to eat."

"I'd judge you if you *didn't* eat with your fingers. It's wings. No other proper way to do so."

"So, tell me about yourself, Nick," I say, changing the subject from eating.

"Basics are, I'm twenty-eight, and my brother, Kaiden, and I opened The Tap House a few years back. He's a couple years older than me and just got married earlier this year to Katie. She was the server running around the bar when you've been in. Pretty low-key guy. Just trying to make a living and enjoy life. The bar keeps me pretty busy, but it's successful, and we've been able to slowly add in more and more staff as the demand of customers require it. How about you?" he asks as we pull into a parking spot.

"Well, you already know about my shitty week. I'm twenty-five, live with my mom in her rundown apartment, am currently jobless, and don't really know where or what I'm doing with my life right now. I'm sure if you looked up the words *hot mess* in the dictionary, you'd find my name and picture right next to it."

"Hey, life hands us all a shitty hand or two. It's how we learn from it and move on that helps us grow and figure things out. Trust me, life hasn't always been sunshine and roses for me, either. The bar gave me something to focus on and be proud of when I needed direction in life," he tells me, then jumps out of the truck and comes around to open my door.

He leads me into a dive of a restaurant, one I would have never known was tucked into this little back corner of the building it's located in. The spices hit me as soon as we walk in the door and my mouth starts to water at the incredible smells.

"They have every level of spice you can imagine, so pick wisely," he tells me as we approach the counter to order.

"What do you normally get?" I ask as I read over the menu.

"A bucket of the medium, with blue cheese dipping sauce and a pitcher of beer."

"How spicy is the medium?"

"Eh." He shrugs his shoulders. "It's got a good kick to it, but I guess it really depends on what you consider spicy."

"And you can eat an entire bucket?"

"Yeah, sometimes I have leftovers to take home, but I usually finish off the bucket."

"Okay," I say, as I take a moment to read over the menu board again. "Since they offer a split bucket, I guess I'll try the mild and the Parmesan Garlic."

"Are you good with Bud or do you want an IPA?"

"I'm good with whatever, plus a glass of water, please."

"You got it," he says as we step forward and place our order with the cashier. She sets the pitcher of beer, glasses of water, and cups for the beer in front of us, along with a number tent to place on our table.

"Do you want to sit outside?" he asks, nodding his head to a door I didn't even notice off the back of the small dining area.

"Sure." I pick up the glasses and pitcher of beer before he can.

I lead the way to the patio area, and we find a smaller table in the corner. Thankfully, the patio is covered, so it provides shade from the bright sun.

"So, are you from Nashville?" he asks, once we're settled at the table and he's poured a glass of beer for each of us.

"We moved here from Memphis when I was a toddler, so it's all I've ever known. My mom has actually lived in the same apartment now for the last ten or so years. Only stable thing in my life has been that apartment." I'm starting to ramble. "What about you?" I ask, trying to turn the conversation off my lackluster life.

"Born and raised," he says, taking a drink of his beer. "My parents still live just on the outskirts of town, as do both sets of my grandparents."

"Are you close, then, with your family?"

"Yes, very. I obviously see my brother and sister-in-law every day, since we own the bar together. But I see my parents and grandparents weekly, or every other week. Not enough, if you ask my mom, but it is what it is. We try really hard to have a weekly family dinner, but with the bar, sometimes that doesn't work out. What about you, do you have much family in the area?"

"Nope," I say, popping the P. I don't elaborate as our food is delivered at that moment.

"Can I get either of you anything else?" the young boy asks.

"I think we're good for now, thanks," Nick answers him. "You were saying," he says, bringing the conversation right back as we both look at the food delivered.

"Just my mom and me. My dad left the picture when I was a baby, I wasn't old enough to remember him. Since then, it's just been a string of one bad relationship to the next for my mom. Not the best role model when it came to what a healthy relationship should look like. Probably why I have a bad habit of picking the ones I do. So, please tell me you're not one of the bad ones?" I say, looking at him with hopeful eyes.

Laughing, Nick looks up from his food and directly at me. His laughter has the sexiest dimples popping out on both of his cheeks that have my insides turning to mush as I look across the table at him. "I'd like to think I'm one of the good ones."

"Phew!" I say, exaggerating the word as I swipe my hand across my forehead. "I guess we can continue this date then. Wait. This is a date, yes?" I ask, hoping I didn't make this more than he was intending it to be.

That damn laugh and those dimples again. "Yes,

it's a date. I guess I really should have thought ahead about where I was bringing you." He looks around at the dive of a place we're at, then down at the food on the table. "Not the best choice for a first date," he says, grimacing.

"It's perfect! I'd much rather be here where we can be laid-back than at some stuffy steakhouse. This is much more my speed." I pick up a wing, looking it over before I sink my teeth into it. The flavor bursts on my tongue and I moan at how amazing it tastes. "Holy shit, you weren't joking. These are the best I've ever tasted," I tell him as I drop the bones in the empty bucket on the table and pick up another one, this time from the other flavor section.

"Glad you like it here," he says as he digs in to his own bucket.

Nick is so easy to talk to, and our conversation flows as we both demolish our respective buckets of wings along with the pitcher of beer. I find myself opening up more with him than I have with any other guy I've dated, and this is only our first date.

7

NICK

Sitting across this little table from Ashley, I watch as she drinks her beer and eats her wings. Coming here was a bad fucking idea. Each moan she makes as she eats has my dick pressing harder and harder against the zipper of my jeans. I didn't realize eating some chicken wings and drinking beer could get me so hard. I don't know if I'm ever going to be able to come here again without this memory coming back to me.

Our conversation has been easy; something I've never experienced with women I've dated in the past. Everything always felt forced or fake. There are only a few women in my life I've been able to talk to with ease —three of them, I'm blood-related to and the other is married to my brother, so definitely not anyone I'd be pursuing a relationship with.

"Have you paid much thought to returning to

school and finishing your degree?" I ask once we've both finished our meals.

"Not really. I'd have to take out more loans to pay for it, and trying to juggle classes and work full-time doesn't sound appealing to me right now. I'm already a mess, I can't imagine how bigger of a mess I'd be if I added that into the mix. Plus, I didn't have the best experience when I was in college before," she says, and I notice right away her demeanor change as she mentions it.

"What happened to make it a bad experience?" I ask.

She looks around and bites her lip, stalling answering my question.

"You don't have to answer that if you don't want to," I say quickly, wishing I could take the words back. I push my chair back before I stand and then offer her my hand. "How about we get out of here instead?"

"Do you work tonight?" she asks as we make it out to my truck.

"Nope, it's my night off."

"Oh, nice. Do you get every Sunday off?"

"Not always. We rotate who works. It's not as busy as Thursday, Friday, or Saturday nights, but when the Predators or the Titans are playing, we tend to be packed."

"That's awesome that you guys stay so busy."

"It definitely helps keep the doors open." I chuckle. When we're both situated, I ask, "Where to now?"

"I'm not picky. If you've got things you need to do, you can take me back home."

"I do have things to do today, but I'm not ready to be away from you just yet," I tell her honestly. "You're easy to be around and talk to. I've enjoyed our time together."

"Same," she says, a smile on her face.

"I've got a few things to get done at my place, do you want to come over?"

"Sure."

I pull out of the parking lot and head for my house, the drive quiet, but comfortable.

"Wow!" Ashley says as we pull into the driveway about ten minutes later. "This place is all yours?"

She looks at my house and I glance out the windshield, taking in my place through her eyes. All I've seen for the last couple of years is the work this place has needed. The blood, sweat, and hundreds of hours I've poured into it to make it what it is today. I'm still not done, but I've made a lot of improvements since I purchased it.

"Yeah, I've put a lot of work into it over the years."

"It's incredible," she says before opening her door and jumping out of the truck.

I follow her lead, then head up the porch steps and unlock the front door. "Come on in, I'll give you a tour," I tell her as she slips by me. I get a waft of her perfume as she walks by me, and it has instantly become my favorite smell. "Living room is to the right, kitchen straight ahead. Both are already done, as they were two of my first projects I tackled."

"Wow! You did all of this?" she asks, turning in a circle as she takes in the space.

"Most of it. I had some help from my dad and brother, and both my granddads helped a time or two, as well."

"This is amazing! You've got a great eye for the aesthetic of the place. A little more decorating and this place would be picture perfect."

"Yeah, I'm not much for decorating. Figured I'd leave that for whenever I settle down, let my wife do the decorating," I tell her, as the thought strikes me. I keep from telling her *she* could be the one to decorate it for me. I'm jumping ahead of myself just a bit. Hell, we just met a few days ago.

"Down the hall are three bedrooms, a full bathroom off the hall that I still need to renovate, and the master has an attached bath, as well. I'm in the process of remodeling that now," I tell her as I show her down the hall and each room.

"What are your plans for in here?" she asks as we enter the master bathroom that is currently gutted.

"A large tiled shower will go here," I say, motioning to the wall where I've started to prep for tile to go in. I point to another section of wall. "A double vanity on this wall, with two mirrors, and a linen closet here."

"That's going to look so good," she says, looking

around the empty room. "I can almost picture it all now. Have you picked your tile out yet?"

"Yep, it's all out in the garage. I'll show it to you next. I also have the vanities and flooring in the garage, as well. Just need the time to start putting everything back together. Once we hire another bartender, I should have some extra time on my hands to work on things here."

"How long have you had it torn out for?" she asks as we turn to leave the bathroom.

I rub the back of my neck, trying to think back. "Probably six months."

"Wow, I'm sure you'll love it once it's done then."

"It will be nice, that's for sure. It sucks having to walk down the hall just to go to the bathroom when I first wake up," I say on a laugh.

"I'm sure it is," she replies, rolling her eyes at me.

We head toward the garage, where she takes in all the building supplies, tools, and all the other crap I've got stored out here.

"You weren't kidding when you said you were doing everything yourself. It looks like a home improvement store out here."

"Yeah, I've got pretty much everything I might need, yet I still make a thousand trips to the store each time I tackle finishing a project because I've inadvertently forgotten something important."

"I've never tried to renovate or build anything," she says absentmindedly.

"It can be a lot of fun. The next time I'm going to work on something, I'll let you know, and you can come help me. I've already demoed everything that needs demoed for now, but taking a sledgehammer to things can be quite the fun project and a bit therapeutic."

"Really! You'd let me help?"

"Sure, why not?" I say, shrugging my shoulders. "As long as you don't burn my house down in the process, I don't think you can do much damage."

"No fires, got it," she says, saluting me.

"Here's the main tile for the shower," I tell her, handing her a piece. "And this is the accent piece," I add, handing her that one, as well. "I'm also going to do a backsplash above the vanity with the tile so that it all matches."

"This is beautiful tile. Did you pick this out?"

"I'll admit I had help from my mom and Katie." I put the tile pieces back in their appropriate boxes. "Here's one of the vanities," I say, pointing to the box.

"Oh, wow! I love that. It is going to look so good with the tile!"

"Credit goes, once again, to my mom and Katie," I tell her. "I basically told them to pick things out and to tell me the total."

She bumps my arm with her shoulder. "That's a lot of trust you have."

"I'd trust those two women with my life," I tell her honestly and turn so we're facing each other, standing toe to toe, with only a few inches between our upper bodies.

Standing this close, I get another whiff of her perfume and it goes straight to my head. I've wanted to kiss her since the first night we met, but it's never been the right time. I start to move closer, our bodies being pulled to each other as if we're magnets. "I'm going to kiss you now, unless you tell me to stop," I say, my voice coming out raspy.

I hesitate just a second longer, giving Ashley the chance to stop this. Instead, her fingers curl into my t-shirt and pull me that last little bit to her. Our lips collide and the world stops. The background of my garage and all the building supplies disappear. In this moment, it's just her and I.

I slide my hands around her sides, one landing on her lower back and the other up and into her hair, stopping at the base of her head. I angle her head, allowing me better access to her mouth as I deepen the kiss. Her lips part at the first swipe of my tongue as I seek access to her mouth. I pull her flush against my chest with the hand against her lower back and can feel my dick harden against her stomach.

The kiss goes on as we both explore each other. Ashley's hands are still buried in my t-shirt, holding on like her life depends on it. I finally break the connection, bringing our foreheads to rest against each other as we both suck in air. "Damn," I say. "Now that was one hell of a first kiss."

"I'd have to agree. I don't think I've ever been kissed like that," she says, bringing her fingers up to feel her well-kissed lips.

"Gives me a bar to meet and try and exceed then, I guess," I tell her, dropping a quick peck to her lips before I step back slightly, allowing a little bit of space between the two of us.

"I guess so," she says, a small smile filling her swollen lips. I snag one of her hands in mine, linking our fingers.

"Come on." I tug on her hand. "I've got a few other things to show you before the tour is finished."

We head back inside and then out the sliding glass door off the kitchen and dining room. "This was my second project," I tell her, motioning to the deck. "I love sitting outside after a long day at work, drinking a beer or grilling, and having friends or family over for a summer barbecue. Growing up, my parents were always entertaining friends and family, and it's something I always loved, so I made sure I had the ability to do so when I bought my own place."

"Sounds like some fun times," she says, looking around like she's picturing what it would be like for this space to be filled with people. "I didn't go to my first barbecue until Tiffany met her fiancé and he had one. Now they have them all summer long."

"You've been friends with her for a long time?" I ask, pulling her back into my side.

"Longest friend I've had. We met in elementary

school and have been connected at the hip ever since. She's been by my side through everything. The good and the bad. Especially the bad," she says, reaching up and quickly wiping a tear from her cheek.

"You want to talk about it?" I ask, not wanting to push her.

"Not really," she says. I've noticed she tenses up or freezes whenever the possibility of what she considers the bad comes up.

"Okay. I'm here if you ever need someone else to talk to," I tell her honestly. I've never been one to discuss feelings, but something has me wanting to know everything about Ashley. I feel an incredible pull to her, one that has me wanting to protect her and ravish her, all at the same time.

"Thanks for the tour," she says a few moments later. "What did you need to get done today? I don't want to keep you from whatever it was."

"Just some things around the house. Laundry, dishes, groceries. It's my day to be an adult," I say, laughing.

"Well, don't let me keep you," she says, stepping out of my hold. I follow her back inside the house.

"Feel free to turn on the TV. I'll go get my laundry started and then we can figure out what to do next."

"We could work on your bathroom," she suggests, the excitement in her expression fucking adorable.

"We could," I agree. "You might get dirty. Are you sure you want to work in what you're wearing?"

She looks down at what she's got on, then back up at me. "Do you have some shorts and a t-shirt I could change into?"

"I'm sure I could find something," I tell her, ignoring the dirty thoughts running through my head about her wearing my clothes.

I head down the hall and into my bedroom. I grab my hamper of dirty clothes and toss them all into the washer after I toss in a couple soap pods, then return to my room and rummage in my closet. Just then, I remember Katie left some clothes here that she wears when helping out.

I cross over to one of the other bedrooms and rummage around in the dresser drawers until I find a pair of shorts and a t-shirt. They aren't mine, but better than Ashley ruining the clothes she's got on.

"Here ya go. I remembered Katie had left some things here from when she's helped out in the past. These will probably fit you better than anything of mine," I tell her, handing over the clothes.

"You sure she won't care?"

"Nope, she's pretty laid-back. She'll be happier that she isn't the one having to help," I say on a laugh.

"Okay," she says, accepting the clothes and flashing me a huge smile. "I'll go change, then be ready to work."

"I'll go gather some tools and supplies," I tell her as she walks down the hall and disappears into the bathroom. I force myself to head into the garage and start gathering things we're going to need. Laying tile is easiest with two people, so I figure we can start with that. I've already got the wall all prepped, so we just need to measure everything out, apply the thin set, and then start attaching the tile to the walls.

"Can I help carry anything in?" Ashley asks, when I bring in an armload of supplies.

"Sure. We're going to tile the shower, so can you pick up a few stacks?"

"Absolutely." She follows me back out into the garage. It takes us about ten minutes to get everything inside, between the dozen or so trips back and forth. We stacked the tile where the vanities are going to go, separating the main tile from the accent pieces.

"Okay, so we have to measure everything out first." I grab the tape measure and long level. "Since I'm adding in the accent pieces, it's important we keep everything level and aligned," I instruct as I start making marks on the wall.

"That makes sense," she says, watching me carefully as I finish up the marks I need.

"Now we can apply the thin set, and then comes the tiles," I tell her as I open the bucket of thin set. "You can use this to apply it to the walls, we just want a thin layer of it like this." I demonstrate how to apply it, and how much to apply.

"Looks easy enough," she says as she gets to work on one of the smaller walls while I tackle the larger wall. It doesn't take us long to have the thin set done and ready for tiles to start being placed. We laid them out on the floor to make sure I liked the pattern and to make sure it was correct. It's a pain in the ass to remove the tile to replace pieces if I fuck it up and put it up wrong.

"Okay. If you want to hand me the pieces one at a time, I'll get them attached."

We fall into an easy rhythm, Ashley handing me tiles and my attaching them to the wall. It only took five or so before she started adding the thin layer of thin set to the backs of the tiles for me before she handed them over.

"Are you sure you've never tiled a shower before?" I ask about halfway through the project. "You're a natural at this."

"Nope, never. Must be beginner's luck or something," she says, a huge smile on her face. I take in her appearance. She's got thin set smeared on her cheek, and dust from helping carry in the materials and from just being in the bathroom and around the unfinished walls, yet she looks beautiful.

"What?" she asks, looking down at herself. "Something wrong?"

"No, nothing." I shake my head at the thoughts running through my mind. "Just wanted to say thanks for helping me," I say, as I lean forward and bring my lips to hers. The tile that had been in her hand hits the floor, breaking as it does so.

"Shit!" she says against my lips.

"Don't worry about it, I've got plenty extra," I say before I forget about the tiles and recapture her lips. She's sitting on a stool and I'm on my knees on the floor, so our positioning isn't the greatest for kissing, but I make do until she pulls back a minute or so later.

"We should probably finish," she says, motioning to the wall.

"Yeah." I sit back on my haunches and blow out a big breath. "You're a little distracting," I say before I grab a new tile from the box to replace the broken one.

"I have no idea what you're talking about," she says, a shit-eating grin on her lips.

"Sure, you don't." I lean down to kiss her once more before I get back to work on the wall.

An hour later, I stand and stretch my tired back as I look at all we've accomplished today. The shower is completely tiled and will be ready for grout in the next day or so. "Thank you for all your help," I tell Ashley as we look over our accomplishment together.

"It was my pleasure. I had a lot of fun," she says, leaning into my side. I wrap my arm around her shoulder and pull her closer. "When will you grout it?"

"Maybe tomorrow or the next day. Just depends on how much time I've got and how much I can be away from the bar. Mondays and Tuesdays are usually pretty slow, so it shouldn't be a big deal if I'm not around as much, as long as Kaiden or Katie are."

"Can I come help again?" she asks tentatively.

"Sure, if you're not busy."

"I don't have any plans. Unless I get called back for an interview by some miracle."

"I'm sure you'll get a call back. Anyone would be lucky to have you work for them."

"Charmer," she says, nudging my ribs with her elbow.

"Not trying to charm you. If you had even a tenth of the focus on your job as you had helping me, any employer would be a fool not to hire you. Like I said, if you have any interest in being a bartender, you could come work at the bar."

"Wouldn't that be kinda weird to work together?" she asks, scrunching up her nose as she looks up at me.

"Why's that?"

"Never mind," she says, as her cheeks flush pink.

I tighten my arm around her. "Tell me."

"It's nothing," she insists.

"It's something, or else you wouldn't have asked."

"Fine," she says, blowing out a breath. "Wouldn't it be kinda weird for us to work together if we're doing this?" She motions between the two of us and it dawns on me what she's getting at.

"Dating?" I question, knowing that's exactly what I'd like to happen between the two of us.

"Yeah," she agrees with me. It isn't lost on me she hasn't been able to say the word.

"If we make it weird. Katie and Kaiden work together and are now married. Granted, they were together before we opened the bar, but it was never a problem for the two of them. Now, what would suck is, the point of hiring another bartender is so that we can have more time off, and that would have you working when I'm off. So, on second thought, no, you don't want to come work for us," I say on a laugh. "It would be a horrible idea."

"I'll probably end up with a job at a restaurant serving that has me working similar hours as you," she says. "Just not usually as late as the bar scene."

"We can take it slow, see where things go," I suggest.

"Sounds good," she agrees. "Slow sounds perfect. I don't have the best track record when it comes to relationships, so I'm sorry in advance if I screw this up."

"Don't be so hard on yourself. We've all made mistakes in the past. But I'm going to guess it was more the *guys* in your past that made the mistakes than you. Take your ex, for example. He's the one that was cheating on you. That isn't your fault. That's all on him. Any asshole that would make you feel like his cheating was your fault is just trying to make you feel guilt, and try and push his decisions onto someone else. *He's* the only one responsible for those decisions, not you."

"Where did you come from?" she asks, looking up at me with a look of astonishment. "I've never met a man like you."

"Nothing special about me, Ash. But I also know how to properly treat a woman and promise that I'll always treat you with respect, always stop when you ask, let you set the pace of this. I'm not here to pressure you into anything you're not ready for. I take that shit seriously. So, if this is too much for you, tell me now, because once I make you mine, I don't think I can hold back."

Moisture builds up in her lashes. I reach up, cupping her face and wiping the tears from her eyes. "I hope one day you'll tell me who hurt you. I already want to beat the shit out of them for it, and I don't even know who the bastard is or what he did to you. But I know someone has hurt you and I promise never to do the same."

I place a soft kiss on her cheek as I hold her close, letting the silence surround us.

"I was raped in college. It's why I dropped out." Her whisper fills the room, and my body stiffens as I hold her tighter against me.

"I'm so fucking sorry," I say in apology as my blood boils.

"Tiffany and I were at a frat party. I'd had a little too much to drink and started to feel funny. This guy I'd been dancing with led me into his room and forced me down on his bed. I don't remember much past that. I woke up in the ER. They completed a rape kit, but he used a condom. Thankfully, I didn't contract any STDs or get pregnant, but I felt used and dirty, and like it was my fault for months afterwards. It took me almost two years before I dated again, and unfortunately, it was one bad relationship after the next for the last couple of years. My mom wasn't the greatest example growing up. She's gone from one loser to the next. Many who abused her, abused me."

"Fuck," I seethe as I hold her tighter. "I'm so sorry that happened to you. Did they ever charge the bastard?"

"Hardly. He got off with a slap on the wrist. It was his word against mine. He came from money and I didn't. His parents swooped in and brought their high-priced attorney. The DA did what they could, but they played dirty and used my home life growing up against me. Tried to make it look like I targeted him because of who he was, who his family was. Tried to play it off as if I was a gold digger, looking at a big payout, when that was the farthest from the truth."

"What a fucking asshole."

"It was bad. He was very popular on campus, so everyone knew about what was going on. I was constantly being harassed by people to the point that I couldn't go to class without being attacked verbally or spit at, bumped into hard enough to knock me over, or at least knock whatever I was carrying out of my arms and onto the ground. I even had professors who turned a blind eye to the way I was being treated, not to mention how my assignments were being graded. I filed a complaint with the university and was allowed to withdraw without being given failing grades."

"I am so sorry you had to live through all of that. I

don't blame you for not wanting to go back to school." The rage I'm feeling for what Ashley went through all those years ago has me wanting to go out and find the motherfucker who did this to her and teach him a lesson, give him the beatdown he should have received behind bars. "Does the bastard live around here?"

"No," she says, her voice small as she holds me tight. "He was from California, and as far as I know, he moved back after he graduated. Tiffany kept tabs on him for a while, but she hasn't mentioned him in a long time, knowing that I don't really care to hear anything about him. As long as I don't ever have to see him again, I've managed to move past that time in my life. I saw a therapist for a little while after, but had to stop going when the funding ran out from the nonprofit that helped pay for my visits. I couldn't afford the visits on my own but was thankful for all the help they were able to provide."

"I'm glad you were able to get help. I can only imagine what it was like to go through all of that."

"It's made me a stronger person, for sure. If money wasn't an issue, I'd go back to school—somewhere different—and get a counseling degree, then open up a nonprofit that provides counseling to abused victims. Not just rape victims, but for women and men who have been in abusive relationships, kids who have been abused by parents or other relatives, family members, et cetera."

"That's amazing. I hope your dreams come true

one day," I tell her as I squeeze her shoulders, then push her back slightly so I can make eye contact. "I know we haven't known each other for very long, but I already know you well enough to know you'd be fantastic at it. Think of all the people you could help."

8

———

ASHLEY

OPENING UP TO NICK ABOUT MY PAST WASN'T something I'd planned to do. I don't like talking about it, but he made me feel so safe. I couldn't not tell him. If anything serious is going to happen between the two of us, he should know.

"How about some dinner?" Nick suggests as we finally pull apart. "I've worked you hard enough today, the least I can do is feed you once again."

"I could eat," I say, just as my stomach rumbles loud enough for both of us to hear.

"I guess so." He laughs. "What sounds good to you?"

"I'm easy," I tell him, then realize how bad that sounded. "I mean, I'm not picky. Whatever you want to have is fine with me."

"I know what you meant," he says, still laughing at

me. "How about I order some pizza? We can watch a movie before I take you back home."

"Sounds good," I agree. "But only if you order me a pizza with Canadian bacon. But no pineapple," I add, grimacing.

"I thought you were easy?" he teases.

"I am, but pineapple doesn't belong on pizza," I say, smacking his abs. "*Ever.*"

"Got it," he says, snagging my hand and holding it against him. "Anything else you'd like on your pizza?"

"Nope," I tell him, popping the P. "Just Canadian bacon and I'm good."

"All right," he says on a drawl, then slips his cell out of his pocket and taps away at an app for a minute. "Pizza should be here in a half hour. How about we head into the living room and find a movie to watch?"

"What types of movies do you like?" I ask, once we're situated on the couch together.

"Comedies, mostly, sometimes a good action flick will interest me, how about you?"

"I don't usually watch many movies, but when I do, I tend to gravitate toward comedy, as well, followed closely by a good romance or drama."

"I love movies. Growing up, Kaiden and I would go to the movies almost every weekend together."

"Sounds fun. Have the two of you always been close?"

"Yep, my best friend since I can remember. We had a few years that we annoyed each other more than we liked each other, but nothing more than just normal brother shit. He hated having to include his younger brother in stuff, and I hated the fact that he was older and got to do shit I didn't. But once we were both teens and past the adolescent stage, we were pretty inseparable. It sucked when he left for college and I was still in high school. I moped around for the first month or so after he left."

"That's great that the two of you are so close. I always wanted a sibling. Tiffany is the closest thing I ever got to having a sister."

"I wouldn't trade anything in the world for my brother. Our close bond has sure helped with our business relationship, as well."

"I bet. Whose idea was it to open a bar?"

"Both of ours. We knew we wanted to be our own bosses, and he has a business degree, with a minor in accounting. I dropped out of school after I got my associates degree in business. Didn't feel the need to continue on to my bachelor's degree when I was going to be focusing on the front of house side of things. When the city started the revitalization of the downtown area, and offered up the tax breaks to businesses, we knew that was going to be the perfect location to open up, and man, were we right. It took us a few months to renovate and get things so we could open, but we've been busy since day one."

"That's so awesome. I bet it was scary opening your own bar in such an up-and-coming part of town."

"Knowing that so many other businesses were committing to the area, as well as developers for housing, we were optimistic that it would pay off, and it sure has. We were profitable within our first few months of opening."

"Have you guys thought of opening other locations?"

"We considered it, but we're happy with keeping it just the one spot. Part of our appeal is the location. We get the patron looking for a laid-back place to grab a drink or two with some friends after work, the young couple looking for good, affordable food that isn't a drive-thru, and we get the sports enthusiasts, looking to watch the game while surrounded by others looking to do the same thing."

"That's awesome that you guys can cater to so many people."

"It really is, and it's one of the reasons we've been so successful." He pauses. "So, you and Tiffany have been friends since you were little, correct?"

"Yes. We met in second grade, when I started at a new elementary school after yet another move my mom and I made. We've been inseparable since. Thankfully, when we moved again after that, we stayed within the school boundaries, so I didn't have to switch schools."

"What does she do for a living?" he asks.

"She's a second grade teacher, and her fiancé is an engineer for the Department of Transportation."

"Cool, have they been together for a long time?"

"They're high school sweethearts, have known each other most of their lives."

"When are they getting married?"

"Late September. Tiffany wanted a fall wedding, which doesn't bode well with a teaching job. So, they're getting married on a Saturday and that following week is fall break, so they'll have a week to take a honeymoon."

"Oh nice." Just then, the doorbell rings and he gets up to answer it. "Hungry?" he asks a few moments later, as he sets the two pizza boxes down on the coffee table in front of us.

"Starving!"

He walks over to the kitchen and looks in the fridge. "Can I get you something to drink? I've got pop, water, beer."

"What kind of pop do you have?"

"Pepsi, Sprite, or root beer."

"I'll take a root beer," I tell him as I open the two pizza boxes and inhale the garlic-infused, carb-loaded yumminess that is in front of me.

"Here ya go." Nick hands me the bottle of root beer, along with a couple plates and napkins. I place two slices of pizza on a plate and hand it over to him, then do the same with my own.

"Thanks," we both tell each other at the same time.

We dig in to our pizza, both apparently starving, as we forgo any conversation until we've both finished our first two pieces, and both reach for a third slice.

"Guess we worked up an appetite," Nick muses as I place the pizza on my plate, then take a drink of my root beer. It tastes really good and I look at the label.

"Like it?" he asks, tipping his own bottle in my direction.

"Yes, what brand is this?"

"I brewed it myself."

"Really?" I ask, impressed, then take another drink.

"Yep, I started brewing my own a few years ago. I've brewed a few beers, as well. If we ever expand, it's something that we want to add to the bar. We'd have to brew off-site and bring it in, as we don't have the space available to install all the equipment that would be required to make large batches."

"That's so neat. I've never tried a home-brewed drink before."

"I've perfected this one over the years. My first batch was horrible. I had to dump it all out, it was so vile," he tells me on a laugh. "Thankfully, with time and some experimenting, I've figured out the perfect recipe for this one, along with a few beers that I like making."

"I'll have to try one of those next time," I say, before finishing off my root beer.

"That you will." He leans over and crashes his lips against mine. "You drive me wild," he says against my lips.

I pull back and look him in the eye. "I could say the

same about you," I tell him as I trace his face with a fingertip.

"Do I need to get you home?" he asks, breaking the contact and looking down at his watch. "I've monopolized your day and evening. I don't want to keep you if you've got things to do."

"I'm good. I don't have a job to go to tomorrow, remember," I say, shrugging.

"I'm sure that will change this week."

"I sure hope so," I tell him as he pulls me against his side.

"If you don't need to go, we can watch that movie we talked about earlier."

"Don't you need to go to bed soon?"

"I'm good. I don't usually go to bed until two or later. Kinda comes with the territory of closing the bar. I'm up later than that on Friday and Saturday nights, so I try not to get my schedule off by too much on the other nights, if I can help it."

"Have you always been a night owl?" I ask as Nick starts to rub my shoulder.

"Pretty much." He laughs. "You?"

"Not as late as you, but I'm usually up until at least midnight."

"Well, tell me when you're ready to go. Until then, I'm going to enjoy having you here," he tells me, then drops his lips to my neck. As soon as his lips make contact, goose bumps break out all down my arms and legs, and sends a bolt of electricity straight to my clit. "You cold?"

A smile crests his lips that are still hovering just over the skin right behind my ear.

"Mhmmm," I moan as his lips return to my skin.

As Nick explores my neck, I turn in his arms, then slide onto his lap until I'm straddling him. I trail my hands up his chest and neck until I cup his face, then bring his lips from my neck to my own, letting him take the lead once we're kissing once again. I can feel him hardening beneath me, and I rotate my hips as I seek the connection I so desperately need all of a sudden.

"Slow down, babe," Nick says against my lips, and I still in his lap.

"What's wrong?" I ask, pulling back even farther, sliding off his lap, suddenly embarrassed I climbed into his lap and was practically dry humping the man.

"Nothing, babe. I just don't want to move too fast for *you*. Just like the other night, I didn't want you making a decision after drinking all night, and right now, I don't want you moving things faster than you're comfortable with."

"I wouldn't have climbed on your lap if I wasn't comfortable with where things were going," I tell him, still embarrassed.

"Shit," he curses. "I didn't mean to make you uncomfortable. I just didn't want you to think I expected sex tonight."

"I didn't think that at all," I tell him, as he pulls me back into his lap and brings my face to his.

"I'm sorry for fucking this all up. It wasn't my intention. I won't stop us anymore, as long as you promise me that *you* will stop me if things go too fast."

"I promise," I tell him before crashing my lips against his once again.

9

NICK

I'M SUCH AN IDIOT. I HAVE A FUCKING GORGEOUS woman on my lap, who obviously has no issues with what we're doing, and I slam on the brakes. Talk about being my own damn cock blocker.

"*I promise*," she told me just a few moments ago, and I have to believe she means it.

I deepen the kiss, pulling her upper body flush with my own. I can feel her stiff nipples through the layers of our shirts and her bra, and I want nothing more than to feel them against my fingers or my tongue. It's been too damn long since I've been with a woman, and having one here in my lap has me ready to rip our clothes off and sink inside her. I just have to get out of my own damn head that she wants the same thing.

Ashley breaks our connection and leans back. "I

think you should take this off," she says, tugging at my t-shirt.

"Is that so?" I drawl, then lean forward and let her drag it up my body and over my head.

"God, I love your muscles," she says as her hands roam over my exposed skin.

"Glad you like them." I flex a little, causing a giggle to slip out of her lips. "I think you should lose this," I say, fingering her top. She immediately reaches down and pulls it over her head, leaving her perfect breasts on display just below my eye level. I lean forward and nip at the tops of them. "Your tits are perfect."

"Glad you approve." She laughs as she reaches behind her back and unsnaps her bra, and I watch it fall away. I suck in a breath as her nipples come into my view and I can't keep myself from giving them each a lick before sucking one into my mouth. *Fuuuck... I'm in heaven.*

"So, I take it you're a breast man?" Ashley laughs as I lavish both of them, rolling her nipple between my fingertips as I suck on the other, switching back and forth.

"I'm a simple man, just in love with the female body," I finally tell her, once I pull back slightly from her chest. I pull her head back down and place a chaste kiss on her lips before I move on to her neck, where I find all sorts of places that have her grinding against me once again. My cock presses hard against the zipper of my shorts and if I'm not careful, I'll be coming in my shorts like I'm a fifteen-year-old boy fooling around with his first girlfriend.

"Nick," Ashley moans as I nip at her neck.

"Yes, Ash," I murmur against her skin.

"Take me to bed. I need you inside me."

"You're sure?"

"Positive," she says, reassuring me. I can see the desire in her eyes and can hear it in her voice. Not needing to be told again, I stand up and her legs instantly wrap around my waist as her arms circle my neck. She latches on to my neck, her lips teasing me as I quickly take us into the bedroom.

I lay her down on the bed, then crawl up and hover over her. I take my time as my eyes rake over her body. "Fuck, you're beautiful," I tell her before I drop my lips to hers in a demanding kiss.

I break away and trail my tongue down her exposed skin, covering her collarbone and down between her breasts, then nip at the sensitive skin on the underside of her breasts. I continue my torture down her torso until I reach the waistband of her shorts. I kiss along it as she squirms underneath me, popping the button of her shorts, then look up to make sure she's still with me, that she still wants this between us.

Seeing the look of desire in her eyes, I continue my perusal and unzip her shorts. "Lift up your hips," I instruct before tugging them off and down her legs. I leave her panties in place, not wanting to rush things.

With her shorts off, I kiss from her knee to the apex between her thighs, but don't touch where she really wants me to yet. I place one kiss on the top of her mound that is still covered by the cotton of her panties, then push back up her body and capture her lips with mine once again.

With my tongue exploring her mouth, I slip my fingers beneath the elastic of her panties and through her slick folds. I circle her clit as she squirms beneath me, her own hands exploring my body as we enjoy each other.

"Ah!" she shouts out once I finally take pity and apply direct contact to her clit, then insert two fingers into her pussy. Her body immediately contracts around my fingers as I push them inside her.

"Fuck, you're tight, baby," I growl into her ear, slipping my fingers in and out of her as I bring her to orgasm.

With the flood of endorphins rolling through her bloodstream, I remove my fingers from her pussy and push myself back and off the bed, where I drop my shorts and boxers to the floor. I give my very hard cock a few tugs before I reach over to the nightstand and pull out the new box of condoms. I tear off one packet and toss the others on the tabletop. I open the packet and roll the condom down my shaft, giving it a few more strokes.

"Bring that impressive cock over here," Ashley says, biting her lower lip as she watches me stroke myself. She's removed her panties and is circling her clit with her fingertips. The vision in front of me has my cock leaking pre-cum.

"Impressive, huh," I say, cocking an eyebrow at her. She's a fucking goddess laid out naked on my bed. The vision of her like this, touching herself as she waits for me, is going to be burned into my memory for years to come. I'll think back to this exact moment, I'm sure, many times while releasing some pent-up energy in the shower.

"Mhmm." She moans, beckoning me closer with a crooked finger. I close the distance between us as I crawl back onto the bed. I drop my head between her legs and lick up the center of her. "Gah!" she cries out when my tongue connects with her sensitive clit.

I suck it between my lips as I slide my fingers back inside her and when she starts to convulse against my tongue and fingers, I move up her body until I'm hovering over her. I look down at her once more as I align my cock with her entrance. When I push my cock inside her, I capture her mouth with my own, plunging my tongue inside her mouth just as I thrust inside her tight-as-fuck pussy.

"Holy shit." I moan as I seat myself fully inside her. "You're so fucking tight, I'm not going to last long," I say against her lips.

"Then you better make it hard and fast," she replies with a smile.

I do just as she asks and find a fast and hard pace

that has both of us cresting over the edge as our orgasms hit hard. I collapse down on top of her, covered in sweat, and bring my lips to her neck as I suck in large gulps of air.

"That was incredible," I say, placing a kiss on the tip of her nose once I've caught my breath, then slip out of her. I roll off the bed and head down the hall for the bathroom to dispose of the condom and to grab a washcloth for Ashley.

When I return to my bedroom, I find Ashley under the sheet, curled up on one of my pillows. The vision of her in that spot has me wishing I could see her right there every night. *Where the fuck did that come from? We've only known each other for a few days.* I shake my head, trying to dislodge that thought. It's way too fucking early for me to be thinking like that. Hell, I don't even know if this thing between us is going to go anywhere.

"You should join me," Ashley says, pulling me from my thoughts as she lifts the sheet and pats the mattress.

I hand her the washcloth and slide in next to her. She gives it back once she's finished and I toss it toward the basket I have in the corner. I hear it *thud* against the floor, but let it stay there. It can wait. I pull Ashley closer to my side and slip my arm around her, settling my hand against her hip as she curls a leg over mine, and we both melt into each other and the bed.

"Did you want me to take you home tonight or

would you like to stay here?" I finally ask as I feel sleep trying to pull me in.

"Would you care if I stayed the night?"

"I wouldn't have offered if I didn't want you to stay," I tell her, winking.

"Then I'll stay." She snuggles in closer. "Your bed is much better than mine," she says on a yawn.

"Is that all I'm good for?" I ask as I bring my fingertips up her side, causing her to wriggle against me and giggle. Her squirming has my cock stirring back to life under the sheets.

"That's not all, but it's sure a perk." She slips a hand around my cock. "You're also pretty damn good with this," she tells me as she starts to leisurely stroke my shaft.

"God damn, woman, you're going to be the death of me. I don't have that quick of a rebound time," I tell her as she works me over.

"We'll see about that." There's a sultry tone to her voice and before I can stop her, she pulls back the sheet and slips down, taking my cock into her mouth. My hands instinctively grip her hair, pulling it all into my fist to keep it from falling into her face, and my eyes roll back in my head as she works my cock over. Her other hand cradles my balls, rolling them as she brings me to a frenzy.

When the tip of my cock hits the back of her throat and she moans around it, I nearly lose my control, but clench my teeth and hold off my orgasm from spilling down her throat.

"I'm going to come," I grit out, but she doesn't stop, so I hook a finger under her chin to get her to pop off my cock. "I'm about to..." I trail off just as my orgasm hits and cum jets from me all over her hand and my stomach. "Come," I finish, once I'm done spilling over us.

"Come here." I pull her up my body, trying to be careful to not make a huge mess, and capture her lips in a demanding kiss. "You're going to kill me," I say against them.

"Not going to happen," she says on a laugh. "But I do need to go clean up."

"We both need to clean up, so how about we just take a shower?" I suggest.

"Mhmmm... that sounds perfect." She drops a chaste kiss to my lips before she gets off the bed.

I follow her out of bed and down the hall to the bathroom. I can't wait for my master bathroom to be finished.

"Here's a towel," I say, handing her one from my bathroom linen closet.

"Thanks, can I have a second one for my hair, please?"

"That's going to cost you," I tell her, a smile on my face.

"Is that so?" She steps in close to me, walking two fingers up my abs and across my chest. "What's the cost?" she asks as she slips her arms around my shoulders.

I bring my lips to her neck, sucking on the sensitive area just below her ear. "A kiss."

"I'm sure that can be arranged," she says on a light moan. I pull back and reach into the closet to grab another towel, placing it on top of the other one resting on the countertop.

I make quick work of turning on the water, letting it warm up for a minute before stepping under the stream, then hold my hand out for Ashley to follow me.

"Can you turn it up?" she asks as she moves under the water. "I like it hot." She runs her hands over the top of her head, directing the water down her hair and back. I reach around her and turn the water up a little.

"How's that?" I ask, already feeling the water scald my skin.

"Perfect. It's not too hot for you, is it?" She bites that bottom lip again.

"I'll be fine," I tell her, standing so the water doesn't hit me much.

"You can turn it down if it's too hot. I know I like it hotter than most people."

"As I said, I'll be fine." I slip my arm around her waist and pull her into me. "I've got you to protect me from it," I say on a laugh.

"Okay," she says before I kiss her.

"I only have guy shampoo and body wash, but you're welcome to use it."

"I don't mind smelling like you," she says. "I rather like the smell of you, so it can't be that bad."

I grab the shampoo and squirt some into her open palm, then do the same to my own. I lean forward and place my head under the water, thankful it's cooled off some since first turning it up for her. I stand back up and wash my hair as she does the same with her own, then wait while she rinses and steps out of the way. I watch as she washes her body—how easily her hands slip over her curves, how easily mine could do the same, and my cock stirs at the sight. I push those thoughts from my mind. We need to cool things off for the night, give our bodies time to recover from tonight's activities.

We finish up in the shower and quickly get dried off. Back in my bedroom, I grab a clean pair of briefs from my dresser drawer. "Would you like a t-shirt to sleep in?"

"Yes, please," she says as she finds her panties on the floor and slips them on. I pull a t-shirt from a drawer and hand it over to her. It swallows her up, but damn, does she look good in my clothes. I'm thankful Katie had clothes here for her to wear earlier as I don't think we would have gotten any work done in the bathroom otherwise. Just something about a woman in my clothes that could bring me to my knees.

"Did you want a toothbrush?"

"If you have an extra one, that would be great," she says, then follows me back into the bathroom. I rummage under the sink and find one, handing it over. "Thanks." She grabs my toothpaste tube from the counter and we stand next to each other, so domesticated as we brush our teeth.

"Do you work tomorrow?" she asks once we've settled back in bed. She's slid right back into my side, with my arm wrapped around her and my hand covering her hip.

"I need to go in for a little while to help Kaiden with paperwork, but I'm not scheduled to tend bar. You want to get together for dinner?"

"Sure," she says on a yawn, snuggling in closer before drifting off to sleep. I look over to the clock and see it's already two in the morning. I didn't realize so much time had already passed by tonight. I let sleep claim me as I hold her tight in my arms.

"Morning," a sleepy voice says, as I stir next to Ashley.

"Good morning, beautiful." I roll over and hover my mouth over hers before I steal a morning kiss. "Did you sleep okay?"

"Yes!" she says, then stretches. I watch the rise and fall of her chest. Even with my t-shirt covering her, I can see the outline of her perky tits under the fabric. "Best night of sleep I've had in a long time. Helps that I had such a warm body to cuddle up next to," she adds before laying her head back on my chest. I wrap my arm back around her and pull her in close, then pull the sheet and blanket back up over us.

"I should get moving for the day," I finally say, a few minutes later. "Kaiden will be calling me soon if I don't show up on my own."

"I know. I should probably get home myself. Need to get back out and apply for some more jobs today. I can't stop until I get one."

"I'm sure you will soon," I tell her, placing a kiss on the top of her head before we both move to get up.

I get dressed in some cargo shorts and a t-shirt. The June weather is in full force, and I'll probably be moving cases of beer around in the stockroom, which always gets me sweaty. "Ready?" I ask once Ashley joins me out in the living room.

"Yep. I'll just grab some coffee once you drop me off," she says.

"We can stop somewhere and grab you some."

"No, that's okay," she replies, and I feel like a flipping idiot. I know she said money is tight right now with her not working, and here I just suggested stopping and spending money she doesn't need to be spending.

"If you change your mind, just tell me. My treat," I tell her as I pull her into my arms.

"I'm good, really. I can get some at home. My mom never runs out of coffee." She squeezes me back, then lifts up on her toes and kisses me.

We break apart and I grab her hand, linking our fingers as I lead her out of my house, stopping briefly to lock the front door. I escort her down to my truck, opening the passenger door, and help her up before I round the front and climb in myself.

"Do you remember the way?" she asks as I start up the truck.

"I remember." I reach over and link our fingers back together. "What time do you want to do dinner?"

"I'm flexible."

"I know you are," I say, winking at her.

"Stop it!" she says, smacking my shoulder with her free hand as she laughs. "I don't care. Five? Six? Later? What time were you thinking?"

"I'll be done at the bar by mid-afternoon, so whenever. How late do you think you'll be out applying for jobs?"

"Who knows. Probably until late afternoon. I need to call this temp agency I found on a sign in the mall, see if they have any jobs I could possibly do."

"How about you call me once you're done for the day and we can make plans from there. Or you could just head over to my place once you're all done. I should be home. I might even head straight home from the bar and start grouting the tile."

"That I can do. Text me when you head home, I might call it quits early and come help you."

"Okay," I tell her as I pull into the parking lot of the apartment building. "Want me to walk you in?"

"You don't have to. I know you need to get to the bar. Just don't forget to text me." She leans over and kisses me before she opens the door and jumps down.

"See you later," I call from my open window as I watch her walk away from me. *Damn, this girl has turned my world upside down in less than a week.* I wait until she's in the building before I back out and head for the bar.

"About time you dragged your ass in here," Kaiden says as I take a seat in our office.

"It's not that late," I say, as I drain the water bottle I grabbed from the bar before I came upstairs.

"You're usually here by ten. It's a quarter past eleven." He looks me dead in the eye. "Oh shit," he says, a shit-eating grin on his face. "Someone got laid, finally."

I just shrug my shoulder at him, as I do my best to keep from breaking out in a smile.

"That girl from the other night?" he asks.

"I don't 'kiss and tell', brother, you should know that."

"I'm not asking for the dirty details, just who the lucky lady was," he says pointedly.

"Yes, the girl from the other night. Her name is Ashley and we hit it off. I'm seeing her again tonight. We had lunch together yesterday and ended up spending the rest of the day and night together. She's like no other woman I've met. Sweet. Feisty. Smart. Has had a shitty hand dealt to her but has made the best from her circumstances, and is trying to better her life, even with being knocked down, time and time again."

"That sucks that she's had such a rough life."

"Yep, it does. She told me about some of the shit she's been through and I wanted to kick multiple people's asses for her."

"Fuck, you're that serious about her already?"

"I can't explain it, Kaiden. She just pulls me to her. Has since the first night I met her and she was crying in one of the booths."

"I get it, man. I felt the same way when I first met Katie. Sometimes, when you meet the one, you just have to go with it. You can't always explain it, but don't fight it like I did."

"I'm obviously not, since all I want to do is be with her. I don't even care what we're doing. Hell, yesterday, she helped me tile the entire shower in the master bathroom, and had fun doing it."

"That's awesome, man. I know you've been wanting to get that done. Finding a woman who just fits into your life so easily is a plus. Sounds like she isn't one of the high-maintenance ones nor a drama queen, who needs all the attention on herself."

"Not at all. She's so laid-back and easy to talk to," I tell my brother honestly. I feel my phone vibrate in my pocket, so I pull it out to check who's trying to reach me.

ASH

I got an interview this afternoon at 2. I'll call you when I'm done. Wish me luck!

That's awesome! Good luck, whoever it is will be lucky to have you. Can't wait to hear how it goes. Where is it at?

It's with the temp agency I called. They have a receptionist position they need to fill for a client.

That's awesome, Ash! Good luck!

Thanks! ;) I'm rushing around trying to get ready for it. I'll text or call you later.

I slip my phone back in my pocket and look up to see my brother staring at me from across the desk.

"Damn, boy, you are a goner."

"So what. You're the same damn way with Katie," I tell him.

"Did I hear my name?" my sister-in-law says as she walks in the office, Starbucks cup in hand.

"Just reminding this one," I say, pointing at her husband, "that he is putty in your hands. He's giving me shit over a girl."

"Oooh... tell me more," she says, rounding the desk and sitting on Kaiden's lap.

"I'm seeing someone, her name is Ashley. You met her the other night."

"I got that much," she muses. "Hey, hands off. You said you didn't want anything when I offered," she says to Kaiden as he tries to steal her cup.

"That's because you always share with me," he says, pretending to pout and she gives in, laughing as he takes her cup.

"Okay, can we get down to business?" I ask, breaking up their moment.

"Yep." Kaiden kisses his wife quickly, then helps her stand and hands back her coffee cup.

"I'll leave you boys to take care of things. I'm going to go get some stuff done at home. I want to meet this girl, get to know her outside of the bar. Make sure she's good enough for you," she says to me.

"I'll see what we can do. Maybe the four of us can do dinner sometime soon."

"Sounds like a plan. Wednesday night would work for us," she says, pointing between her and Kaiden.

"I'll see if that works for her schedule," I say to her retreating back, then turn back to Kaiden, all-business. "Okay, so how was the weekend?"

"It was a good one. I've got the sales data already input into QuickBooks and am working on the deposits. We profited a few grand this weekend, a nice increase over last weekend, as we've successfully done the past six weeks in a row. We're on par to more than double our income this year. I'm really happy with our success. The advertising we've done has really been paying off these last few weeks. We should have done it a long time ago, but we can't turn back time now."

"I'm glad to hear that this weekend was so profitable. It sure was busy in here on Friday and Saturday night."

"I've started putting together the ad we talked about last week to start advertising for the open bartender position. I'd like to get that filled sooner rather than later, if we can. We might even consider hiring two new people, and another server for the floor for the busy nights."

"Can we afford all that?" I question Kaiden.

"I wouldn't be suggesting it if we couldn't. None of those positions would be full-time, so no benefits would be provided. But I think having more staff will help eliminate the stress on us some and will allow us to serve customers that much faster, which will help us attract more patrons. Word of mouth will get out, and I think we'll continue to see an increase in our profit, even with the additional payroll. We might take a hit at first, but I think it really is the best move for us."

"You've obviously crunched the numbers, and you've never led me wrong with them thus far. So, I say we go ahead with your plan and look to add three new employees."

"I knew you'd see things my way," he says on a laugh.

"What are your thoughts on us looking into finding a space to start the brewery portion of our business? I was talking to Ashley about it a little last night, and that got me thinking about it again. I know we'd put it on our five-year plan, but with how well things are going, do you think we could move it up?"

"Potentially. Can you pull together a rough estimate on what it will cost us to get it up and off the ground, and we can see how things look after we've hired the new employees? Get basic costs on everything, from the rent of space to all the equipment and ingredients to get the first batch going."

"That, I can do," I assure him, excited our business is doing so well and that we might be able to move forward with the part I'm most passionate about. "Did you have anything else to go over with me?"

"Nope, that was all."

"Sounds good, I'll get you those numbers pulled together. For now, I'm going to go move stuff around in the stockroom so it's ready for the delivery tomorrow morning."

"I'll come help you," he says, pushing back from his desk and standing.

"Thanks."

It takes us an hour or so to move all the stock around and get everything ready for our weekly order to arrive. "Looks like we went through a lot more rum this past weekend than we anticipated. I'll call and see if we can add to our order for tomorrow," Kaiden says once we're done.

"Yeah, we had that large party order two full bottles on top of what we normally go through. I'm thinking that we should add a pre-order option for large parties like that. Gives us the heads-up that they're going to want bottle service so we can make sure we've got the stock on hand."

"I like that idea," he says, nodding. "I'll pass it on to Katie as a suggestion. I'm sure she'd agree to it. Then we can have her give us a heads-up whenever we've got a party booked, so we can add their order to the delivery, if necessary."

"Sounds like a plan. If we've got nothing else going on around here, I'm going to take off. I need to grout the shower today, if possible."

Kaiden pulls me in for a quick man-hug. "Get out of here. I'll see you tomorrow."

"I'll talk to Ashley about dinner on Wednesday and text you later."

"Good idea. You know if you don't, Katie will be on your ass until you do." He laughs.

10

ASHLEY

"Thank you so much, Ashley, for coming in today on such short notice. After looking over your application, I thought you might be the perfect candidate for this open position one of our clients is desperate to fill," Jackie, the owner of the temp agency, tells me after I'm seated in her office.

"Not a problem at all, thank you for calling me back and in for an interview."

"So, I know you've mostly worked in the restaurant business as a server, but I see here that you've taken some college courses and noted that you have an interest in counseling. Can you tell me a little bit about that interest?"

"Sure! When I first went to college, my plan was always to get my degree in Psychology. Some things happened that derailed my plans, but my desire to help people overcome their difficulties is still there. I haven't had the opportunity to return yet to finish that degree, but one day, I will."

"That's great. The reason I ask is because the open position is for a counseling office. They are looking for a long-term employee. The placement is a conditional placement, meaning that for the first thirty days, you'd be an employee of the temp agency. If, after that period, both you and the HR manager feel like you're a good fit, you'd be offered an employment contract directly from them and, if accepted, would transition to be a direct employee of their company."

"That sounds amazing," I tell her before we launch into more basic interview questions for the next twenty minutes or so.

"Well, Ashley, I think you'd be a great fit for this job. The hours are normal business hours, for the most part—Monday through Thursday, eight a.m. to four thirty p.m., with a half-hour lunch. On Fridays, they are open from eight a.m. until one p.m. The pay through us is eighteen dollars an hour, and they would like me to fill the position as soon as tomorrow, if possible. What do you think? Is this something that would interest you?"

"Absolutely! And I can start tomorrow."

"That's great. I'll alert the HR manager, Mandy, and send over your information. I'll print you off some information on the company and where to report to tomorrow morning. The dress code is business casual, and they allow jeans on Fridays," Jackie tells me.

I'm so excited I've been offered such an incredible job, I'm about ready to bounce out of my seat. But I keep it together, knowing I can freak out once I get out to my car.

"Here you go, dear," Jackie says, handing me a piece of paper a moment later. "I'll have to fill out the direct deposit and W-4 paperwork before you leave here today, so that we can get you entered into the system for payroll. We pay on a weekly basis, so your first paycheck will be for whatever hours you work this week. Our pay weeks are Monday through Sunday and are paid the following Friday of each week, so you'll get your first paycheck next Friday. Mandy will send me your hours, so you don't have to worry about that."

"Thank you so much. I can't tell you enough how much this job means to me. I won't let you or Mandy down," I tell her wholeheartedly.

"That's what I love to hear. As I said before, I just have this feeling that you're going to be the perfect fit for this position."

"Thanks for that confidence. I really appreciate this chance," I tell her one last time before she sees me out of her office.

"Susan, can you please give Ashley, here, the new hire paperwork? She'll be filling the receptionist position for Healing Touch Counseling." Jackie addresses the receptionist in her office, then turns back to me. "Ashley, it was great to meet you, and please call me if you have any issues with the placement."

"Thank you, it was nice to meet you, as well."

She retreats back to her office, and Susan hands me a clipboard with a few sheets of paper on them.

"Just bring these back to me once you've finished them and you'll be all set. If you don't have a paper check to void, the routing and account numbers, along with the bank name, will be just fine for the direct deposit part."

"Thank you." I take the clipboard and then find a seat in the waiting area. It only takes me a few minutes to complete the paperwork and hand it back to her. I can't keep the huge smile from my face as I leave the office and head for my car.

I drive straight for Nick's house, and am thankful his truck is in the driveway when I pull in. I'm still on cloud nine about my job and want to tell him in person. As soon as I park, I shut off my car and beeline it for his front door. I know we had a great time together yesterday, but I don't feel like I can just walk into his house, so I knock loudly while ringing the doorbell at the same time.

I'm bouncing on the balls of my feet when he finally opens the door.

"Hi!" he says in greeting, pulling me into his arms. "How'd the interview go?"

"I got the job!" I squeal into his ear. "Sorry, that was a bit loud," I apologize after he winces.

"That's awesome, babe!" he says, squeezing me tighter. "Where is the job at?"

"Healing Touch Counseling, as their receptionist. I start tomorrow!"

"That's great, I'm proud of you! We'll have to celebrate for dinner tonight," he says, setting me back down on my feet.

"Sure. I'll just need to call it a night early, since I need to be well-rested for work tomorrow. I start at eight."

"Do you want to stay here again tonight? We could stop by your mom's place and pick up what you'll need for tonight and tomorrow. I'll promise to let you sleep tonight," he says, a devilish look on his face.

"Sure, you will." I laugh as I smack his chest.

"I promise I'll be good. I just know you said that my bed was more comfortable than yours, and I sure didn't mind having you in it last night," he replies, leaning in and kissing my neck.

"You sure know how to convince me. Dirty tactics, sneaking in and kissing my neck," I tell him as I squirm against him.

He grins. "Just trying to win you over, baby."

"I guess you've convinced me," I tell him a moment later, then notice he's kinda dirty. "What were you doing before I showed up?"

"Grouting the shower. Did you want to come see what I've done so far?"

"Yes! Anything I can help with?"

"Nope, especially not in those clothes." He points to what I've got on. "I'm almost done anyways, so there isn't much that you could do. Just sit in here and keep me company," he says as I step into the bathroom.

"Nick," I say, "it's beautiful! I can't wait until the entire room is done. It's going to be incredible."

"Thanks. We'll have to christen it once the grout has dried and can get wet," he says, winking at me.

"I look forward to it," I tell him, and the look in his eye tells me he wishes that moment was right fucking now.

I sit on a bucket in the corner, away from the grout, and watch as he finishes up the last bit, which takes him about twenty more minutes. "I think that does it," he says, standing back up after setting his sponge down. He twists from side to side, stretching his back from being bent over and working.

"It looks really good. Is your back bothering you? Need me to massage it for you?"

"Just a little sore. I'm not used to being crouched down like this for so long. But I'll never turn down having your hands on me," he says before bending down to kiss me.

"Of course you wouldn't," I say against his lips.

"What do you want to do for dinner? I can grill us something or we can go out. Whatever you want. We're celebrating you tonight."

"I think you cooking for me sounds perfect. Time to impress me with your culinary skills."

"Oh, I'm here to impress," he says, squeezing my hip. "Let's go grab what you'll need for tonight and tomorrow, and then swing by the store to pick up some steaks for me to grill."

"Sounds like a plan." I stand and follow him out of the bathroom, then sit on the edge of his bed and watch him strip his work clothes off before pulling a clean t-shirt and pair of shorts on.

"You're drooling," he says, looking over at me with a smirk.

"I am not," I state, then wipe a hand across my lip, just to make sure.

"You could have been, and I made you check," he says, cackling as he approaches the bed where I'm perched. He crowds my space, boxing me in as he places an arm down on the bed on either side of me. "I think someone was enjoying the view in front of her." He brings his lips to my cheek, then moves over to my neck, and nips at my earlobe.

"Maybe." I moan slightly at the sensation his lips against my skin evoke.

"Maybe, my ass. Someone was ready to strip out of her clothes and climb me like a tree," he replies against my skin as he nips at my neck.

"Okay, Mr. Cocky." I push him back gently. "Enough of that. You promised me some dinner and if we don't get a move on, I have a feeling that we'll never get out of here."

"I promise to feed you before I make you scream my name later."

"Someone is sure full of himself," I say on a laugh.

"You'll be full of me later, baby. That, I can promise," he says, then helps me stand, wrapping his arm around my waist. He slaps me on the ass then kisses me hard on the lips. "Let's get moving."

We head out to his truck, stopping at my apartment first.

"Hey, Mom," I say as we enter the apartment.

"Glad to know you're alive," she states from her spot at the table in the kitchen.

"Sorry." I know I haven't really kept her informed as to when I was going to be home lately, not that I even knew myself. "Mom, this is Nick. Nick, this is my mom, Donna."

"Nice to meet you, ma'am," Nick greets her, holding out his hand.

"Nice to meet you," she replies as she accepts his hand. "You the reason my daughter hasn't been home much since moving in?"

"Guilty as charged," he tells her, a smirk on his face.

"I got a job today," I tell my mom, changing the subject, which brings her attention back to me.

"Ashley, that's great news! Where at?" she asks.

"Healing Touch Counseling, as a receptionist. I got it through a temp agency that I applied with."

"Is it a long-term position?" she questions, and I tell her everything Jackie explained to me earlier today.

"I'm proud of you," she replies, when I finish. "I hope it works out well for you."

"Thanks, Mom, I'm excited for it. I start tomorrow. They needed someone as soon as possible, so it was a perfect fit, and Nick is making me a celebratory dinner tonight because of it. We just stopped by so I could pick up some things that I'll need for my first day."

"Have a good night, then. Call me tomorrow and tell me how things go on your first day."

"I will," I promise my mom and then take off for my room. I grab a small duffel bag and toss in some lounge clothes, some panties and bras, a couple t-shirts, shorts, and a pair of jeans, before I rummage through my closet and pull out the few business casual outfits I have. I'll have to get creative with mix and matching the items until I can afford to buy some new clothes.

"Need any help?" Nick asks as he sits on the bed, watching me toss everything into the bag.

"Nope, I'm good," I tell him, remembering to dig through my closet for a few pairs of shoes. One last trip into the bathroom to grab my makeup bag and toiletry bag and I'm ready to go.

I get everything to somehow fit into the duffle and zip it closed. "I'm all ready. I figured I'd bring a few extra things, just in case I end up back at your place tomorrow night or later this week," I tell him, as my cheeks pink.

"I like that idea. Saves us from having to come back over here again tomorrow," he says, tugging on my pockets until I'm standing between his spread legs. His hands slide around my hips as he grips them. I lean down to meet him for a chaste kiss before pulling back.

Back in the kitchen, I give my mom a hug. "Have a good night, Mom. I'll call you tomorrow after work and let you know how it goes. Love you."

"Love you, too, sweetie."

"ARE YOU SURE YOU DON'T NEED ANY HELP?" I ask as I sit on a chair on Nick's deck an hour or so later, while he mans the grill. I'm nursing another one of his homemade root beers that are quickly becoming my favorite drink.

"I've got it all covered," he assures me. "Not much to it but flipping things when they need to be flipped." He does just that and flips the steak, vegetables, and potato wedges he has all lined up on the grill. "If you really need to do something, can you run in and grab a platter, two plates, and some silverware? We can sit out here and eat tonight."

"Sure can," I say, hopping up from my seat. I stop to give him a quick kiss before I head inside and find everything we need.

11

NICK

I watch as Ashley disappears into my house to grab the plates and silverware. I admire the swing of her hips as she does and wonder how we can just click so easily together. How, this time last week, we'd never crossed paths and, as of today, I don't want her to leave my side. Fuck, I'd be happy if she just moved all her stuff into my house and called it good. I know that isn't an option yet, but damn, if it doesn't feel right to have her here in my space, cooking dinner together and just living life.

"Here ya go," she says, pulling me from my daydream, then sets the plates and silverware out on the table. "Do you need anything else?"

"Nope, this is all," I tell her before turning back to the grill to remove the food.

"Oh my god, this steak is amazing," Ashley moans a little while later, as she takes a second bite.

"Thanks, I've perfected grilling over the years. I do a lot of it, with only cooking for one most of the time. I can only eat so much bar food before it gets old."

"I bet. Have you always enjoyed cooking?"

"Not really. I don't necessarily enjoy it, just a necessary part of life. Once I was on my own, and realized quickly that I couldn't survive on takeout and freezer meals, and the leftovers my mom likes to send me home with after a meal at my parents' house only lasts me a day, if that. The only thing I miss about living at home is my mom's cooking. What about you, are you much of a cook?"

"I guess so. I've been cooking since I can remember. I don't usually go all fancy, but I've got the basics down and can put a well-rounded meal on the table. I'm also the queen of making entire meals out of the random things I can pull out of a pantry. Sometimes money was super tight, and we'd have very little to get us by until the next payday or food pantry date. Even after those days, it was still sometimes a meal pulled together from a mish-mash of random items from the pantry and freezer. If I never have to eat another bag of frozen mixed vegetables, it will be too soon."

"I can't even imagine what it must have been like to go through days like that," I tell her honestly. I never had to wonder where my next meal was coming from, and I'm thankful for that every damn day.

"The ironic part about it was that for most of my childhood, I didn't even realize that we were poor.

Since all my friends lived in the apartments all around us, I didn't know better. I try and focus on the happy moments more than the crappy ones."

We fall silent as we focus on eating and not talking. The flavors from the fresh grilled vegetables and steak are bursting on my tongue and satisfying my hunger.

We finish up eating and work together to get our dishes cleared and into the dishwasher. I tried to insist I didn't need any help, but Ashley wasn't having it.

"Thanks for helping clean up. You ready to relax some before you need to go to bed?"

"That sounds perfect," she says, stopping in front of me and lifting up on her toes to kiss me.

I cradle her face between my hands, loving the feeling of her soft skin against my callused hands. "Or, I could take you to bed now," I say against her lips before I dive back in for another demanding kiss. She wraps her arms around my waist, closing the small amount of space left between our bodies.

I have no idea how much time passes as we stand here in the kitchen, exploring each other. We're a mess of lips and tongues, teeth occasionally clinking together. I eventually slide my hands down her body until I can grasp her thighs just under her ass.

"Jump," I instruct, breaking the kiss for a second as I hoist her up into my arms, then place her down on the counter. I make sure her ass is close to the edge and step between her legs, pulling us close together.

I trail my hands along her hips and then under the

fabric of her top. My fingertips brush along her skin, as I slip higher and higher up her body. "You can take it off," she whispers next to my ear.

I don't need to be told twice, so I grab the hem of her shirt and pull it up and over her head. My eyes drop to the roundness of her tits on display for me in her lacy bra before I start covering the pillowy tops with open-mouthed kisses. Ashley arches her back as she pushes her chest further into me. I slip a hand around to her back and easily open the clasp of her bra. I stand back long enough to remove her bra completely and toss it behind her on the counter, out of our way.

"Your tits are perfect," I growl, just before I suck one of her nipples between my lips. I lightly bite the tip, then run my tongue over it to soothe the sting. I switch to the other, where I do the same, which causes Ashley to moan in frustration.

"We need to move this to the bedroom," she says, pulling my head from her tits.

"I could fuck you right here," I suggest, a smirk on my lips.

"You could," she muses, reaching for the button on my shorts. They drop to the floor a second later, followed by my t-shirt and boxer briefs. I pull her shorts and panties down her legs, then lean over and grab my wallet off the counter, pulling out the condom I keep in there, just in case. "Let me," she says, grabbing the packet from my fingers as I toss my wallet back on the counter.

I watch as she tears the package open and then rolls it down my shaft. The contact of her hand to my cock has me ready to bury myself inside her. Once the condom is in place, she strokes up my cock from the base to the tip.

"That's enough," I growl. "I need inside you now."

I slip my fingers through her wet folds, sinking two fingers inside her pussy to make sure she's wet and ready for me, then tug her ass to the very edge of the counter, line myself up, and thrust inside her.

"Fuck!" I yell. The heat. The wetness. The all-encompassing feeling I get when I sink inside her. It feels like home. Like this is where I belong. Like she's my forever.

"Lean back, hold yourself up with your hands, baby," I tell her as I grab her hips. Once she's supporting her upper body, I start thrusting. I watch as my cock disappears inside her, only to come out covered in her. The sight has my blood boiling and my orgasm quickly shooting down my spine.

I move one hand from her hip so I can strum her clit with my thumb. "I need you there, babe. I'm not going to last much longer," I tell her as I speed up my ministrations. I feel her walls start to pulse around my cock as I drive into her, harder and as deep as I can get.

"Yes," she hums and her legs lock around my hips as I pump faster and faster. I work at hitting her g-spot, all while still strumming her clit. "Ahhh!" she finally cries out a few moments later, and collapses forward, wrapping her arms around my neck and bringing her upper body flush with my own. I thrust through her orgasm until I'm spilling my release into the condom.

I rest my forehead against her shoulder as I suck in large amounts of air. The counter isn't the greatest height for sex, so I soon slip out. I take care of the condom, then come back to stand in front of Ashley. Her body is still flush from her orgasm. She pulls me back between her legs, wrapping them, along with her hands, around my body.

"That was..." She trails off as I kiss her lightly. "Perfect," she finishes once our kiss ends.

"It was," I agree, a dopey smile on my face. "Are you ready to call it a night?"

"It's only eight thirty. How about we watch something for a little bit? I'll head to bed closer to ten."

"Sounds good to me but, babe," I say, looking down at her still-naked body, "if we're going to *actually* watch TV, then you need to put some clothes on."

"I know that," she says on a laugh. "Same goes for you."

Ashley pinches my side, then pushes me back so she can hop off the counter. She picks up her clothes that are either on the counter behind her or on the floor with mine. "You coming?" she asks as she turns to head for the bedroom.

I pick up my own clothes and follow like a puppy behind her. We toss our clothes into the basket in the corner, then pull out some lounge clothes. I laugh a little when we both pull on some athletic shorts and a tank top.

"What's so funny?" she asks as she grabs her toiletry bag from the larger bag she packed earlier.

"Just that we practically match. We already think too much alike," I muse, pointing back and forth between us.

"We've both got good taste, then." She smiles, then heads down the hall and into the bathroom. I continue down the hall into the living room, making a quick stop in the kitchen to grab us each a glass of water before I plop myself down on the couch and turn on the TV.

I start scanning the guide as I search for something we'll both like to watch, and see one of the Stanley Cup finals games is on. If I'm not mistaken, the Indianapolis Eagles could win the cup if they beat Columbus tonight. I flip to that channel and find the game is about halfway into the first period and the Eagles are currently winning, one-nothing.

Ashley comes out a few minutes later, her face scrubbed clean and her long blonde hair pulled up in a mess on the top of her head. "Hockey okay with you?" I ask, holding out my hand to her so she can cuddle up next to me on the couch.

"That's fine. I don't know much about it, but that's okay."

"If the team in white wins tonight, then they win the cup," I tell her.

"I'm guessing they want to do that, then?" she asks, obviously knowing nothing about hockey.

I laugh at her lack of knowledge about the sport. "Yeah, something like that. The Stanley Cup is said to be the best trophy in team-based sports. It's the only trophy from the four major sports played in the United States not to be reproduced each year. Instead, it travels from city to city, team to team. Each player from the winning team actually gets a day with the cup during the offseason. They can do whatever they want with it on that day. Many players will take it to local children's hospitals or just have a day with it and their families."

"Cool. So, I take it you like to watch?"

"I'm a lover of most sports. Plus, we play the games at the bar, especially if the Preds are playing."

"Duh." She smacks her forehead with the palm of her hand. "I forgot that you guys play games at the bar on a regular basis. Wait, what just happened?" she asks, pointing to the screen.

"They just scored."

"Wow, the crowd really gets into it."

I once again laugh at her ignorance to the game. "That's because they're one of the hottest teams in the league the past eight or so seasons. And as I said a little bit ago, if they win tonight, they'll win the cup. And they're on home ice, so that stadium is packed full of Eagles fans."

"Do you ever go to games here?"

"I love going to games. We should plan on going to one next season. I think you'll like it. I have a buddy, Ethan, who used to play for the Preds, that I usually go with. He's now a tattoo artist at a shop not far from the bar."

"Sounds fun!" She bounces lightly next to me as she watches the game. "Holy crap!" she says as we watch a defenseman from the Eagles hit a Columbus player against the boards. She turns to look at me. "They can do that?"

"Yep. It's a pretty brutal game sometimes."

"But he just popped back up like nothin' happened," she says, flabbergasted at the play.

Laughing once again, I tug her a little closer. "Just all part of the game. The Eagles are going to do everything in their power to close out the series tonight, and the other team is going to do everything they can to keep the series alive. Keep from ending their season as the losing team."

Our conversation lulls as we watch the remainder of the first period. "This is so exciting," she says, once the game breaks for the first intermission.

"I'm glad you think so," I tell her as I reach for the remote. I mute the TV while the intermission report comes on. "So, are you all ready for your new job tomorrow?"

"Yes. I've got the address already programmed into my phone. I'm going to get up at six, shower, have breakfast, and leave around seven twenty. That should give me plenty of time to drive there, even with morning traffic. The GPS on my phone says it's only a fifteen-minute drive from here, but I know with morning traffic, that can easily double. I also don't want to be late for my first day, so having a little buffer of time will be good, I think."

"Sounds like a great plan," I tell her, then get up and head into the kitchen. I grab a spare key off a magnetic bar I have mounted on the wall, then walk back into the living room. "Here, take this." I hand over the key. "This way, you can lock up when you leave in the morning and you can come back here once you're off work. I'll be at the bar, but you're welcome to come back. I wouldn't complain about finding you in my bed when I get home from work tomorrow night."

"Thanks," she says, accepting the key. "You're sure you're ready for me to have this? Kinda a big step, isn't it?"

"It is, but it makes sense. Especially with our schedules not really lining up once you start tomorrow. You can come and go as you want. Just promise me that you'll be in my bed when I get home on the weekends. It might be late those nights, but I can promise you I'll be ready to sink inside you after my long shifts, take my time making you come." I watch as her breath hitches and I know my words are turning her on. I can see her nipples harden beneath the thin cotton of her tank. My cock swells in my shorts and there's no hiding it.

"I'll think about it," she says, a smirk filling her lips as she looks up at me.

"Don't make me come hunt you down when I get off work Friday night."

"Who says you'll have to hunt me down?" she says coyly. "Maybe I'll come keep you company at the bar. Sit at the end all night, sipping on a drink, eating some nachos, driving you crazy with some low-cut top..."

"Woman," I groan.

"What?" she says on a laugh.

"With you there distracting me, I won't get work done."

"You were just fine the last few times I was in there."

"Yeah, but that was before I knew what it was like to be inside of you. To see your perfect body without clothes on. Before I knew what your nipples and pussy feel and taste like against my tongue," I tell her, then pull her against me and capture her lips in a demanding kiss. She immediately opens to me, straddling my lap an instant later.

We make out like teenagers for a few more minutes, neither one of us able to get enough of the other. If I could keep my lips on this woman twenty-four seven, I would. I'm becoming that addicted to her.

"Game's back on," she says, after we break apart and she looks over her shoulder at the TV.

I grab the remote and un-mute it as we both settle back in beside each other. I watch her reaction as the

Eagles continue to dominate the game. They easily keep control of the lead and finish out with a win. We watch a bit longer as the teams complete the handshake line, then the team is awarded the cup.

"That was so cool how they all shook hands. I've never seen something like that," she tells me while we watch all the guys pass the trophy around as they each take a lap around the ice.

"It's a hockey tradition. At the end of each playoff series, the teams come together and form the handshake line. It's a great show of sportsmanship. These two teams battled it out and unfortunately for one team, they go home the losers and the other team will be out celebrating all night long. Then, in a few days, the home team will have a big parade in their town. In most cities, it draws hundreds of thousands of people out."

"That's pretty cool," she says on a yawn, then looks over at the clock on the wall. "I need to get to bed. It's already past my bedtime."

"Then let's get you off to bed," I tell her, standing and offering her my hands to pull her up.

"You don't have to go to bed with me. I know you like to stay up later."

"I'll be fine. I just want to hold you."

"Okay." She grabs the two glasses I'd brought out here earlier for us and places them right into the dishwasher, then pushes the button to start it.

We both head down the hall, each taking a turn in

the bathroom as we get ready for bed. When I return to the bedroom, she's dropped the shorts and is sliding into bed in just her tank top and panties. My cock hardens at the sight of her ass that's on display in her cheeky cut underwear. I breathe in deep through my nose, blowing the breath out through my mouth as I will my cock to stand down. We've already fucked tonight, and I need to let her get some sleep, so she's well-rested in the morning.

I slide into bed a moment later, and she moves right up to my side, cuddling in. I wrap my arm around her, pulling her another few centimeters closer as we both melt into the bed and each other.

"Goodnight, babe," I whisper into the dark room, a minute or so later.

"Night," she sleepily says, and I can tell a minute later, she's fallen asleep, as her breathing changes and she melts further into me. I scroll through Facebook on my phone while I lay here with her in my arms. She's quickly worming her way right into my life and heart. If I'm not careful, I'll be falling in love and be ready for everything with her before she even knows what hit her.

12

ASHLEY

ONE MONTH LATER

"Nick!" I call out as I step through the front door. I've still got the key he gave to me a few weeks ago, and come and go at my own will. I don't technically live with him, but I'm here more nights than I am at my mom's place.

"I'm back here." His voice sounds like it's coming from the bedroom. I head inside and find him in the master bathroom, tools all out as he finishes installing the new vanities.

"Hey," I say once I reach the doorway. "It looks amazing in here."

I look around at all he accomplished today. We've worked on things here and there over the past month, but it's slow going with my full-time job and his time at the bar.

"Thanks. Figured I should take advantage of the

day off. We can finally start using this bathroom now. Only thing that's left to do is wipe everything down and start putting things away in here," he says, a huge smile on his face.

"So, what I'm hearing is that we can finally christen that shower we worked so hard on a few weeks ago?" I ask him, already able to picture what it will be like for him to pin me against the wall as he fucks me.

"I'm sure we can arrange something like that," he says, a smirk filling his lips.

"So," I say, stalling, a huge smile of my own filling my lips. "I have some exciting news."

"Did they offer you the full-time position?" he asks, an excited look on his face.

"Yes!" I cry out in happiness. "Plus, a raise, and full benefits, including tuition reimbursement, if I want to return to school at some point."

"That's amazing news." He closes the distance between us and swoops me up in his arms, spinning us in circles. "We need to go out and celebrate," he says, placing me back down on my feet before he crushes his lips to mine.

"Sounds good to me. I'm going to call my mom and tell her quick."

"Why don't you invite her to come? I'll call Kaiden and Katie and my parents, and see who all wants to join us to celebrate your big news."

"You sure?" I ask, shocked he'd want to invite so

many people, just because of my official full-time employment.

"Of course. This is something to celebrate. You know my family adores you and they'd love to be included."

"Okay, where should we go?" I ask, trying to think of places that can accommodate a party of at least seven people.

"Wherever you want to go. It's your big news and night."

"How about Mexican? I could go for some tacos tonight."

"Sounds perfect." He looks at his watch. "How about we tell everyone to meet up at seven if they can make it. That will give me time to clean up in here, plus take a shower before we need to leave."

"Sounds perfect," I tell him, sneaking in one more kiss before I head out to the living room to call my mom and then Tiffany to tell her my big news.

We finally arrive at the restaurant and find that everyone has come out and almost all of them beat us here, as we're followed in by Tiffany and Colton. "Thanks for meeting us," I tell everyone once we're all seated at a large table.

"We wouldn't miss it for anything," Barb, Nick's mom says, smiling from across the table.

"Good evening," our server greets us. "Can I start you all out with some beverages? Maybe a couple of pitchers of margaritas for everyone to share?"

"That would be perfect. Let's go with two to start with, as well as a pitcher of strawberry daiquiri," Nick tells him, knowing my dislike of tequila.

"Right away. Would you like any appetizers while you decide on dinner?" he asks. Nick's dad, Donald, orders some queso for everyone to share.

We fall into conversation while we wait for the drinks and appetizer to come, which continues while we wait for our main meals and throughout the rest of our time at the restaurant.

"We're so happy for you," Barb tells me in the parking lot as she pulls me in for a hug before we part ways.

"Thank you. I was so nervous that they weren't going to offer me the position. So, I've been on cloud nine since our meeting at the end of the day today."

"I'm sure they were elated to offer it to you. Sounds like it, if they offered you a raise after just a month," Barb states.

"I know. As I said at dinner, I was shocked about that. But I guess they had to pay the temp agency an even higher rate while I was their employee, so they were able to afford to pay me a little more and still not be spending as much as they were with the agency."

"That's usually how it goes. The temp agency has to make money somehow, and that's how they do it."

"I think I'm most excited about the tuition reimbursement. I've really been thinking about returning to school and getting my degree."

"That's so amazing. You let us know if you need help with any of that," she tells me, and I'm still so shocked at how easily Nick's family has accepted me into the fold, as if I've always been a part of their family.

"Thanks," I tell her, doing my best to hold back the tears I can feel starting to form. I swallow down the emotions as we say our final goodbyes.

"Proud of you," my mom says, pulling me into a hug once Donald and Barb are in their car and pulling away.

"Thanks, Mom," I tell her, hugging her tighter.

"I'm guessing that you won't be coming home tonight?" she asks as we break apart.

"No," I tell her as Nick sidles up next to me, wrapping his arm around my shoulder. "I'm going to go home with this guy."

"No problem. I figured that was your plan. I'm surprised you haven't just moved out yet," she says on a chuckle.

"I practically have. I think ninety percent of my things are already at his place."

"You know, babe, you could move the last ten percent of your things in and just admit that we live together," he says. He's been telling me that now for the past week or so. And it's true. But it also feels like it's way too soon for us to be officially living together. So much for my plans to take a break from men after Chris cheated on me. It's hard to believe that that happened only a month and a half ago. Feels like it was years ago.

"I know," I huff.

I've heard this every day. He's starting to wear me down, but I keep holding out and not committing to it. I don't know why, he's nothing like any of the guys that I've dated. He's completely different, and it sometimes still catches me off guard how sweet he can be to me. How his priority is me. What I want, how I want things, what I think about things. Not what I can do for him or how quickly can I make him come. He doesn't treat me like I'm his live-in maid or cook.

Hell, the guy gets mad when I toss in his dirty clothes and do the laundry while he's at work. He's adamant I don't need to do things for him, and I have to reiterate that if I'm offering, it's because I *want* to, just like he wants to do things for me. We're a team, and the more time that goes by, the more we fall into an easy rhythm together.

The last time I slept at my mom's, I tossed and turned all night, and got the worst night of sleep I'd had in weeks. I missed having his warm, strong body wrapped around me. I missed rolling over in the morning when my alarm went off and kissing him before I slipped out of bed to get ready as quietly as I could as he slept, then kissing him goodbye once more before I left for work each morning.

"I'm off this weekend, we should do lunch together," my mom suggests.

"I'd love that. I'll call you Friday night and we can finalize our plans."

"Talk to you then," she says before retreating to her own car a few spaces down from us.

"Ready to head home?" Nick asks, then places a kiss to my forehead.

"More than ready," I tell him. I'm still feeling good from the two glasses of daiquiri I had with my dinner. Between the nine of us, we easily polished off the three pitchers of drinks he ordered for us as we enjoyed our meal.

Once home, I place our leftovers in the fridge then join Nick on the couch.

"Thank you for tonight," I tell him as I slip into his embrace. He's lying down on the couch and I'm facing him, our chests resting against each other's as our legs intertwine.

"Of course," he says, placing a quick kiss on my forehead as he runs his hands through my hair. I love it when he does that; it's so soothing and relaxing. Lying with him on the couch like this has quickly become one of my favorite ways for us to relax together. It's intimate, and we take the time to talk about anything and everything, from our days, to future plans, as well as things from our past.

"How are the new hires coming along?" I ask, changing the subject.

"They did well last night. I think another week or so and they'll be good to go. Obviously, they'll never be working by themselves, but knowing they could hold things down if that happened is important."

"Are you ready to present Kaiden with all the numbers for starting the brewing center?"

"I think so. I put some final touches on the proposal this morning and am ready to go over everything with him tomorrow. I really think that we can make it work. It might mean we have to make some sacrifices for a little while, but I think that it will quickly start turning a profit once we get the first batch done."

"Are you going to talk to him about switching your focus to just the brewing side of things, now that you've added more staff?"

"I plan to bring it up as something we'll need to work towards. I know I'll need to stay behind the bar for a while, but I think if the brewery side of things takes off like I think it will, I'll need to focus on that as a full-time job. That will be nice for us, as it will bring our schedules more inline. Or at least take out so many late nights for me."

"It would be nice to have you home more on the weekends."

"The late-night weekends have been such a big part of my life for so long now, I don't know what I would do with a Friday night off." He laughs.

"Think of all the things we could do if you were off on a weekend."

"Sorry to break it to you, babe, but those thoughts

will have to wait for a little while longer. Kaiden will want to comb through everything I present to him, crunch numbers himself, and make an educated decision. I can't fault him for how serious he takes decisions like this, as it's important. We wouldn't be where we are today if it wasn't for him being as dedicated to the business and numbers side of things as he is. I sometimes like to joke that he's anal about money, but if he wasn't, then we'd probably be underwater or not even open anymore. Because of his dedication and expertise, we've built ourselves quite the business that we can both be proud of."

"I know, and I'm proud of both of you. He relies on you to keep the front of the house running smoothly like you depend on him to keep the back of the house running. You guys make a good team."

"That we do," he agrees. "So, about that conversation with your mom..." He stalls, kissing the top of my head that's resting on his chest. "Are you ready to give in and admit that you live here?"

I can hear the humor in his voice in the question. He's asked me this multiple times the past couple of weeks, and I've always told him no. But something in my mind has changed tonight and I can't quite put my finger on it, so what the hell.

"Yes," I say into his chest, a smile filling my face.

"Fuck yes." He throws a fist in the air, which has me falling into a fit of laughter. "I thought it was going to take me a few more weeks, maybe months, to get you to admit that," he says, pulling me up so he can kiss me on the lips.

"Just don't hurt me, please. Don't make me regret this," I tell him, the vulnerability coming out, not only in my words, but my voice.

"Ash." He cups my chin, so I'll look up at him. "Listen closely," he says, dropping a chaste kiss to my lips. "I will never, and I mean *never, purposely* do anything to hurt you. I know our relationship has moved pretty fast and we've just clicked. I know we've still got a ton of shit to learn about each other, but there is no one else in this world that I'd rather have beside me in life. There's no one else in my life that I want to celebrate milestones with or have at my side when things aren't going the way I'd planned.

"Before I met you, I wasn't interested in long-term. I wasn't interested in relationships. I was focused one thousand percent on the bar. Now, the bar hours piss me off because they keep me from you so much of the time. I know that I won't be working the hellish hours forever, and because of that, I can deal with it for now. I know *we* can deal with it for now."

He pulls me closer, holding me tight as he continues, "I know the men in your life haven't left you with a good impression on what a real man is like, but I'm here to show you. I'm here to show you that you deserve to be treated like the strong, intelligent, beautiful woman you are. I'm here to show you that you're just as important in this life as I am, and if I'm honest, more important than I am. I'm here to show you that a real man will hold up the woman he loves, not beat her down with his words or fists or actions. I'm here to walk beside you because, Ash, you've changed me. You've cast your spell and made me fall in love with you."

His lips crash against mine and I can feel tears streaming down my cheeks at his words. I don't know what I did to deserve this man, but I'm so thankful our paths crossed when they did. I'm almost thankful for that day I lost my job and found Chris cheating on me. If it weren't for those two events, I wouldn't have been crying in the booth in Nick's bar that first night he helped me. I probably would have gone back a few nights later for Tiffany's birthday, but that connection wouldn't have already been there. That pull we each feel toward each other. It's like we're two puzzle pieces that have finally found their place together.

I pull back from the kiss and look into Nick's eyes. The love I see pooling in his dark blue eyes is everything. I know down to my soul I can trust this man with everything that I am. That he will be my future, my forever.

"I love you," I whisper into the small space between us, looking him straight in the eye. I've never told a man those three little words, but they just felt so right.

"I love you so fucking much," he replies, and the huge smile covering his face is contagious. His thumbs swipe across my cheeks as they brush away the tears that still are flowing freely.

13

NICK

"Morning," Kaiden greets me as I walk into the office and take a seat across from him.

"Morning. How are things around here?" I ask, our exchange pretty typical each morning.

"Good, last night was surprisingly busy for a Tuesday night."

"That's good. Are you ready to go over these numbers on the brewing?" I ask, holding up the binder I've put together over the past month or so.

"Now's great, let me just go refill the coffee cup and I'll be ready."

"No problem," I tell him as he gets up and heads downstairs. While he's gone, I pull out the information, placing his copy on the desk and readying mine to explain everything included in the costs.

"All right, lay it on me," he says, sitting down and opening the binder.

"I've separated everything into categories. First, is the space. I've found a space that I think will be perfect for the setup, and it's not far from here—just a few blocks away, actually. They are willing to discuss a rent-to-purchase option, which I think is beneficial to us, as we'd eventually own the property and would build the equity. Especially if we end up scaling up and add more tanks down the road.

"The next section"—I point— "is all the equipment that we'd need to purchase. I've set it up to have the equipment to start out with being able to brew two batches at the same time, that way we can appeal to a wider customer base."

I pause long enough to take a drink from my water bottle before jumping right back into things. "The third section is the actual brewing supplies we'd need, which are pretty straightforward. The last section is the packaging section. I figure, at startup, we'd only keg it to have at the bar, but if I can dream big here, I'd love to think that, at some point, we could bottle it up and end up on the shelves in stores. I know that piece is a ways off, but I included it, to be thorough."

"This looks great, Nick," Kaiden says, flipping through all the pages as he reads through my notes and numbers.

"Oh, and the last page has a spreadsheet with all the numbers together, color coded even, with things broken down into startup costs, mid-point expenses, and future expenses."

"You really put a lot of work into this," he says, sounding impressed as he flips to the last page with the numbers. "It actually isn't as much as I was thinking it would be for startup costs. What kind of timeframe are we looking at to actually get beer in the bar?"

"The building would need some work, obviously the tanks would need to be ordered and installed. If we got started on everything soon, I'd think we could be brewing within six weeks, maybe eight. Then it would be another six or so weeks after that before beer would be ready. If we give ourselves a few extra weeks buffer for delays, I'd say we'd have beer on tap by the new year, probably earlier than then, but for sure by January."

I can tell he's mulling all the information over as he flips through the information in front of him.

"I know that it's going to be a commitment, and one that we have no guarantee will take off. But, small batch breweries are killing it these days, and I think we can tap into that. With us just having hired some more employees that are all well-versed in handling the bar, I think this is the perfect time for me to be able to swing my focus to this part of the business. I wouldn't completely step back from being behind the bar, but I think that if I'm focusing on the brewing side of things, that most of my time will be spent there and not here."

"I get that, and I agree that our staff can handle things," he says, still flipping back and forth between pages. He's got his super-serious, furrowed brows, look on his face, and I wait in anticipation for his answer. "I think you're on to something with this and these numbers look good. We've got enough in our savings to cover the startup costs, still leaving us a nice cushion for other business expenses. We've also got the business line of credit should anything go wrong."

"So, you're on board?" I ask, trying to keep my excitement tamped down.

"Yes. Let's do it," he says, a huge smile on his face.

"I'm happy to hear you say that," I tell him honestly.

"I see the positives, and you've obviously done your homework and know what you need to do to make this as successful as you can. One thing I'd be interested in from the beginning, is seeing if the building owner would be interested in just selling from the start. We'd have to get a loan for that, but if we're going to be renovating to fit our needs, I'd rather be doing that to a building we own."

"I can find out for sure," I tell him, seeing where he's coming from.

"Let's do that, find out if we can just purchase now, and if so, start the negotiations on the sale. I can call up our banking contact and get the ball rolling on the possibility of a new business loan for the purchase."

"I'll get on it today, and hopefully have an answer for you by this afternoon. Thanks, brother. I think this is going to be something special."

We part ways and I call up our realtor to have him

start looking into the purchase option on the building. Within hours, he's got answers for us and an offer written up for Kaiden and I to look over before he submits it.

"Hey, baby," I call out as I come into the house, finding Ashley on the couch.

"How was your day?" she asks, a smile filling her lips, like she's excited about something.

"It was great. We're moving forward with the brewery. Kaiden loved my presentation and we've submitted an offer to buy the building rather than rent it."

"That's amazing! I'm happy that it's all working out for you."

"Me too, babe. How was your day?" I ask, dropping down to give her a kiss.

"Good, work went well. I stopped at Mom's place after and packed up the rest of my things and brought them here."

"About damn time," I tease her. "What did you want to do for dinner?"

"I've got some steaks and veggies all ready to go, just waiting on you to fire up the grill," she says sweetly.

"Perfect. What would I do without you?" I muse before I kiss her once again.

She laughs. "You'd be eating bar food."

"Touché," I say, laughing with her. "What do you say we get that dinner going. I'm starving."

"Sounds good to me." She stands up and pulls me with her into the kitchen. We grab the food, then head out onto the deck.

"So, I was thinking," she says, pausing to look over at me as I place the food onto the hot grill, "what would you think about getting a dog?"

"Ah, I guess I don't really have a thought about it. I've never gotten one because my hours weren't the greatest to have one. But I'm not against the idea."

"Yay! I've always wanted one, but we could never have one growing up because of living in rentals and, to be blunt, we just couldn't afford to have one. But now, living here with you makes me want one so bad."

"Do you know what kind you want?" I ask, dropping into a chair next to her.

"Not really. I figured adopting one from a shelter would be best. So, whatever one we like the best."

"Sounds reasonable to me. Do you want to go check it out this weekend? Maybe after I get up on Saturday, we can go?"

"Really?!" she asks excitedly, then smiles at me. "That's all it will take to convince you?"

"Babe"—I reach out to run a fingertip down her cheek—"if a dog will make you happy, then I'll gladly adopt ten. Well, many not ten at once, but you know what I mean," I say on a laugh as her eyes widen.

"Where did you come from, Nicholas David Watkins?" she asks before leaning forward and pressing her lips to mine.

"Been here, just waiting on you to sweep into my life."

14

ASHLEY

SIX MONTHS LATER

"Settle down," I say to Max, our mutt of a dog that has been the perfect mix to our little household. It took us about a month to find him after that first day I brought up the idea of Nick and I adopting a dog. Once he's calmed down and sitting nice, I place his treat on the ground in front of him, before giving him the signal he can pick it up and take it to his bed in the living room.

"Hey." Nick walks up behind me and wraps his arms around me, pulling my back to his front. "Are you almost ready?" he asks, kissing my cheek.

"Yep, just need to slip on my shoes and we can get out of here." I turn in his arms and press my lips to his. "I'm so damn proud of you," I tell him before he releases his hold on me. "You followed your dream, and look where it's gotten you."

Tonight, they'll be tapping the first keg from the

new brewery. We've all taste-tested things the past week or so, and even without being a big beer drinker, Nick has done an excellent job with everything. Since the day they closed on the building, he's been making the brewery his work priority, and he's put in a ton of blood and sweat over the past six months, as they brought this adventure to life and hopefully a successful addition to the bar.

"Thanks," he says sheepishly. He's never one for much praise, but he damn sure deserves it tonight.

The drive over to the bar is quiet as Nick is, I'm sure, inside his own head, worried tonight is going to be a bust. I'm convinced it isn't going to be. The bar has had a bunch of local press, and a few of the news stations, as well as the newspaper, have all done segments on the brewery. Plus, Kaiden put together a bunch of promotion, advertising the launch of the new beer tonight.

We pull into the parking lot, Nick parking his truck in his usual spot out back. He brought the kegs over a few days ago and made sure everything was set up and working properly, so they don't run into any snags tonight.

"Hey," I say once we're out of the truck, before we reach the back door. "Just take a deep breath. Things are going to be perfect. You've done a phenomenal job and people are going to love it; I can just feel it."

"Thanks," he says, taking a deep breath before he brings his forehead to mine. His arms go around my body, pulling me into him, and I feel him relax as he does so. "We've just got so much riding on this and tonight."

"I know, and I'm sure it's a scary thought, but it's not a sprint, it's a marathon. You're not going to make everything back tonight, but you can damn well sell a few kegs' worth of beer," I jokingly tell him.

"That's the plan," he says, a small smile filling his lips. He squeezes me lightly. "Thanks for being here tonight with me."

"Nowhere else I'd rather be," I tell him, before I push up slightly on my toes and press our lips together. "Love you," I whisper against them before pulling away.

"Love you, too. Now, let's get inside and sell some beer," he says, pulling me along behind him as we enter the back door.

The bar is already open, but the plan is to not tap the keg until six o'clock, when they make a big deal about it. I follow Nick upstairs and into the office, where we find both Kaiden and Katie.

"Hey, guys," Katie greets us.

"Hey," Nick tells her, wrapping an arm around her shoulder in a half-hug before she pulls away and gives me a full hug.

"Ready for tonight?" she asks him as she returns to her seat on Kaiden's lap.

"As ready as I'm going to get," he says, pulling his baseball hat off his head and running his hands through his hair. The guys ordered some apparel with the bar's logo on it recently, and that included some new hats, which Nick has been attached to since they arrived.

"Quit your worrying," Kaiden tells him. "Everything is going to go great tonight. We've done our research, advertised, had great press about everything, and the crowd has already started to form downstairs, waiting for us to tap that first keg."

"I know," Nick says, blowing out a huge breath. "We've just got a lot riding on how things go tonight. I don't want the venture to fail. We've both got futures to look towards, and this could set us back if it fails."

"Nick," Kaiden says, a sternness in his voice. "We made this decision together. Not just you, but *together*. And it's going to work out just fine." A shit-eating grin appears on his face. "I haven't told you this yet, but I got a call this morning. We've made the finals for an award, on the sample you submitted to that contest."

"You're shitting me?" Nick exclaims.

"No, I'm as serious as a heart attack. I wouldn't joke about something like that. Nick, you've done amazing things with this and we're going to keep doing great things. Believe it. Good things are headed your direction. With the press an accolade like that will bring to us, as such a new brewery, we'll definitely be going places. Even just making it to the finals is an accomplishment in itself. I'm proud of you. I'm proud to have you as my brother. I'm proud to have you as my business partner. There isn't anyone else that I'd rather be in this adventure with than you. Well, maybe these two crazy women, who seem to think that we're worth keeping around, for some unknown reason."

"Thanks, brother. The feeling is mutual," Nick tells him, accepting a handshake and hug from Kaiden.

"Shall we head downstairs?" Katie suggests. "It's almost time."

"After you," Kaiden tells her, and we all file out. Downstairs, the guys take their positions behind the bar, and I join Barb, Donald, and my mom, who have a table already.

"Thank you all for coming out tonight," Nick says to the crowd, who has quieted down to listen to him speak. "We've waited a long time to bring this to market, but we hope you guys enjoy it. And with that, who wants a pint of beer?"

He pulls the tap and fills the first beer. The crowd starts talking all at once, bringing the volume in here up very quickly. I sit back and watch as Nick fills glass after glass, for what feels like hours. They run out of the first keg and quickly get the second one tapped and flowing as the patrons all enjoy the two options they have available for tonight.

"I'm so proud of my boys," Barb tells me, after sampling both beers Kaiden brought over to our table.

"Me too. They work so well together. You did good raising them. I can only hope to be the same way when the time comes," I tell her honestly. With my bad luck with men, kids were never on my radar, but as time goes by and Nick continues to show me what a real man is, my thoughts have been slowly changing and I can see us with kids down the road. Like, a few years down the road.

"Hey, sorry we're late," Tiffany says, sitting down on the empty stool next to me. Colton stands behind her, his hands resting on her shoulders.

"You made it!" I say, wrapping her in a hug. We've not seen much of each other between our busy work schedules, and she and Colton enjoying their newlywed life.

"Yeah, sorry. I wasn't feeling well today, but finally pulled myself out of bed so we could make it down here. We wanted to celebrate with you guys. How's it been?" she asks, looking around.

"Great! They've already had to tap the second kegs on both beers."

"Sounds like I'd better go get one, then, if I want to try them before they run out," Colton says, then turns to Tiffany. "You want anything?"

"Just a ginger ale," she says, smiling at him over her shoulder. He leans in and places a chaste kiss on her lips.

"Be right back," he says against them before heading over to the bar.

"Sorry you're not feeling well. Germs from school?" I ask.

"Nope." A smile fills her lips. "We're pregnant," she tells me quietly.

"Oh my god! Congratulations!" I tell my best friend as I pull her into a hug. "How far along are you? When are you due?"

"I'm about eight weeks, which would put me due in late August."

"Ahh! I'm so excited for you guys. Is Colton excited?" I ask.

"Yes, he's been so sweet these past few weeks while I deal with morning sickness. And I'm so damn tired. I get home from school every day and collapse on the couch. He's been doing everything so I can rest. Cooking, cleaning, bringing me things to keep my stomach happy."

"Aww, what a sweetheart. We already knew he was one, but I'm glad he's stepping up like that."

"Me too. I don't know what I'd do if he wasn't so helpful," she says as he returns to the table.

"I hear congratulations are in order," I say, pulling him into a hug.

"Thanks," he says sheepishly.

"How's it going?" Nick asks everyone at our table a moment later, as he slides up behind me and places a platter down in the center, filled with their appetizer samples. "Thought y'all could use some food to soak up the beer."

"This is great, man," Colton tells him, holding up the beer he's tried first.

"Thanks, that's what I like to hear," Nick says, slapping Colton on the back.

"Looks like I'm not the only one who thinks that," he replies, looking around the packed bar.

"Even better." Nick laughs. "I just wanted to bring over the food and make sure everyone was doing okay, but I'd better get back behind the bar." He leans in and presses his lips to mine. "Love you," he says against them before walking back to the bar.

Nick assumes his place at the tap, filling glass after glass as the orders continue to roll in all night.

Nick

I'VE FILLED MORE ORDERS TONIGHT THAN I CAN count, and I couldn't ask for more. The turnout tonight, the feedback on the product, just the upbeat atmosphere has me feeling like this is an out-of-body experience. I could have only dreamed things would have gone this smoothly. Not one person has said they didn't like the beer we've launched.

Even with filling glass after glass of the two beers—a light blonde I named The Ash and a slightly darker Raspberry Wheat named The Kat. Both beers were inspired and named for the two women in Kaiden's and my lives. Kaiden was on board with my idea from the moment I brought it up to him, and the girls were quite honored when we told them about it a few weeks ago, when we had our first samples of the batches.

I watch Ashley's table from my peripheral vision most of the night. I watch as she visits with her mom and my parents, as well as with Tiffany and Colton. I know she doesn't get to spend as much time with Tiffany as she wishes she could, so I'm glad to see they came out tonight and that the girls are getting some time together.

"Hey, man," I hear a familiar voice call out, and I look over to see my friend, Ethan, and his wife, Cam. "Can I get one of each?"

"Nice to see you guys, thanks for coming out tonight," I say as I slide a pint of each beer across the counter to him and Cam. "How are you guys doing?"

"Great. Looks like a good turnout tonight," Cam says as she picks up the pint and takes a drink. I closely watch for her reaction to it, as I've done with many patrons tonight. But when it comes to my friends, I truly want to know what they think.

"It's been a great one," I finally remember to respond.

"Holy moly," Cam says, as she swaps pint glasses with Ethan. "You have to try this one, it's fantastic. The raspberry flavor is really good." I smile at her assessment of the beer and watch as they each sample the opposite drink. "Nick!" Cam smacks the bar top, grabbing my full attention. "These are fantastic! I think I've found my new favorite beer with that raspberry one."

"I'm glad to hear that. We'll be offering take-home growlers soon," I tell her. "We had a slight delay in getting our bottles in, as the manufacturer had a defect in our first shipment and had to remake all of them."

"That sucks." Ethan sets the glass back on the counter, sliding it back over to me. "I'll take another one of those," he tells me. "How's everything else going? I haven't seen much of you lately."

"Been busy over at the other building with the brewing side of things. But life's been great. How's Ben?"

"Growing every day. I can't believe he's walking and talking already. He gets into everything, but the best thing to happen to us," Ethan says, gushing over his son.

"That's great, man. Glad to hear things are going so well. We'll have to get together soon."

"Let's do that," he agrees.

"Ashley is over there." I point to her table. "If you guys want a place to hang out for a while."

"Thanks, I think we're going to finish these up and head out. Have to go get the boy and head home."

"No problem, thanks for stopping in tonight," I tell him, reaching over the bar to shake his hand.

"Our pleasure. And these are excellent. I look forward to whatever else you come up with."

"Hopefully some more hit flavors. The plan is to have these as two of our signature brews that are available all the time, then add in one other flavor that will be kept to one-batch runs at a time. We had a third set of tanks installed so we can be running a third flavor at the same time."

"When will the first alternate flavor be ready?" he asks.

"Another few weeks or so. That one is a chocolate ale I'm hoping is a hit for Valentine's Day."

"Sounds interesting, but you know I'll try anything at least once."

"I'll make sure to let you know when it's ready. You can stop by the warehouse when we're sampling it before we keg it. Tell me what you think of it then."

"Sure, just text me."

"Will do. Have a great rest of your night," I tell them as they step away from the bar, stopping to say hi to Ashley before heading out.

We stay at the bar until around midnight when the crowd starts to thin. The staff will be able to handle the rest of the night on their own. I'm damn proud of our success tonight, and the weight that has been sitting on my shoulders since we started this venture has started to lift.

"You kicked ass tonight," Ashley says as she lies in my arms in bed.

"Thanks," I tell her, placing a kiss on the top of her head as I run my fingers through her hair. I love these moments when we just lie here, talking about whatever happens to be on our minds at the moment. Talk about our future, our past, failures, successes, our dreams. Anything goes.

"So, I've been thinking of something lately."

"What's that?" I ask.

"I think I want to enroll in a few classes for the spring semester. Start working toward my degree."

"I think that's a great idea. When does that start?"

"In a week. One of the classes I found is offered online, so I can do it whenever, and another one is offered as a night class. It's Tuesday and Thursday nights, from six to eight, so it wouldn't interfere with my work hours."

"That's great. What do you need from me?"

"Nothing. Just your support. It might take us a little bit to get used to my new schedule, and I'll have to dedicate some of my evenings and weekend hours to studying and homework, but I think by limiting myself to taking only two classes at a time, it'll keep me from overwhelming myself between work and school."

"I think that's smart. Start small and work your way up if you find that you can do more."

"I've read over the tuition reimbursement policy at work, and plan to send Mandy an email on Monday to just verify things, but the way I understand it, is that I have to pay upfront for the classes, and upon completion of the class, I fill out a form and provide proof of my final grade. As long as it's a passing grade, they'll reimburse me one hundred percent of the costs, books, and any fees included, up to ten thousand each calendar year."

"That's amazing. With only taking two classes at a

time, I imagine that you'll be able to have them pay for the majority of your degree that way."

"That was my exact thought. And I have enough in savings to cover the cost for the first set of classes, so I wouldn't need to take out any student loans. At least, not at this point."

"You wouldn't need a loan anyway, babe. I've got enough in savings that I could help you out, as well."

"I would never expect you to do that, Nick," she says, propping herself up so she can look up at me.

"I know you'd never *expect* me to pay for it, but I love you and I know how important this is to you. I've got the resources and *want* to help you achieve your dreams."

"You're too good to me." She leans in and kisses me.

"I could never be too good for you. If anything, you're too good for me. I'm the lucky one in this relationship," I tell her as Max attempts to jump up on our bed. I snap my fingers and point to his dog bed along the wall. "Max. Bed." He walks over to it, circling it, before he plops down on it in a huff. If I didn't know any better, I'd think he just told me off.

"You're sure it won't bother you that I'll be gone those two evenings each week, or that I'll be busy on the weekends doing homework?"

"No, and if it did, that would make me the biggest asshole on this planet. Look at how many nights and weekends I've been busy at the brewery these last six months. You've put up with my schedule our entire relationship, I can deal with you being busy following your dream of getting your degree."

"Thank you," she says, shaking with excitement. "I can't believe I'm taking the leap and signing up for classes."

"I'm fucking proud of you, babe. Seeing you overcome your fears and overcoming your shitty past is amazing." I pull her in for another kiss, this time, flipping her onto her back so I can hover over her. I ravish her mouth before moving down her body. I cover every inch of skin I can touch with my lips before I reach her center, which I quickly cover with my mouth. I bring her to the edge with my tongue on her clit and my fingers buried inside her pussy, pulling back as I feel her ready to explode. I wait as her body calms down, only to do the same thing once again.

"Nick! I need to come!" she whines when I release her clit once again.

"Patience." I smirk as I slide back up her body, stopping for a few moments to suck each of her nipples into my mouth. "As much as I enjoy you coming when my tongue is on your clit, I want you coming on my cock tonight," I tell her, tapping the tip of my cock against her clit and watching her eyes as the sensation drives her crazy.

"Then fuck me already," she cries, moving her hips to try and make me slide inside her.

"My pleasure," I tell her, rolling on a condom

before I push inside in one rough thrust. "Fuck." I groan as her hot walls clamp down around me.

I hold myself up, an arm braced on either side of her head, as I pound into her. Her legs are firmly locked around my waist and her fingers dig into the skin of my sides, doing her best to hold on tight as I work to bring us both to the brink. I shift, sliding a hand to her breast, where I tweak her nipples, down her stomach until I'm circling her clit with my fingertips. Her wetness from earlier is still lubricating her clit and I apply firm pressure against it, knowing it will make her detonate any second.

"Yes," she chants. I swear my cock slips deeper and deeper inside her as her hips shift up higher.

"Come for me, beautiful," I tell her as I feel her walls start to contract around me. The tightness has me seeing stars, and I feel my balls draw up in the tightness of my own orgasm. I can't stop it, so I just ride it out, slamming my hips forward one last time, burying my cock as deep as I possibly can, before I collapse forward, doing my best to not crush her under me.

15

———

ASHLEY

FOUR MONTHS LATER

"Hey." Nick's voice pulls me from my laptop. I've been staring at it all morning as I work on the first of my final papers.

"Hi," I say, rolling my neck side to side as I stretch the kinks from my muscles.

"Can you take a break? Maybe have some lunch with me before I have to head to the bar?"

"Sure, let me just finish this sentence and save, and then I can take a break for a little bit."

He leans in and presses his lips to mine for a chaste kiss. "Sounds good, I'll go put together some sandwiches for us. Meet me out on the deck in five?"

"Yes. Thanks." I smile up at him before he walks away, and I return my focus to my computer, finishing up and saving a few minutes later. I hit up the bathroom before finding him out on the deck, with sandwiches, potato salad, and two glasses of lemonade.

"Come sit down and relax," Nick says, patting the seat he has pulled up right next to him.

"I needed this. Thank you," I tell him after I swallow a huge bite of my sandwich. "I didn't realize how hungry I was until you suggested some lunch."

"I didn't want to interrupt you when I got up, but when the clock kept ticking by and you didn't stop, I figured you could use a short break."

"Yeah, that and I didn't eat anything this morning, just jumped right into my homework after I fed Max and made my coffee. I couldn't skip that," I tell him as I take another bite, this time of the potato salad.

"You can't be doing that to yourself," he chides playfully. "No more skipping meals."

"I just wasn't hungry when I first started and well, then I just lost track of time as I was in the groove. Sometimes, sacrifices are necessary. And it isn't going to hurt me to miss a meal or two."

"None of that shit now," he says, a serious note to his voice. "You're perfect just the way you are."

"You have to say that," I tell him, rolling my eyes.

"No, I don't, but it's what I truly believe. You need to love yourself more than I love you, or anyone else loves you. You are an amazing woman, who's beautiful, not only on the outside, but the inside, as well. If you don't love yourself, then you'll never be able to accept someone else's love for you."

"You're truly a wonderful man. I do love myself, and I know I'm strong. I wouldn't have made it this far in life if it weren't for my strength during the hard times. I just wish these five extra pounds I've put on these last few months would go away. You keep feeding me all this good food, and the beer isn't helping," I tell him, poking his chest with my pointer finger.

"If I didn't keep you fed, you'd forget to eat half the time," he says, laughing.

"I'm not that bad!" I protest.

"You kind of are, babe," he says as he finishes off his sandwich.

"Ok, maybe I am. So, sue me."

"I'll just keep feeding you instead." He winks at me. "How late do you think you'll be working on homework today?"

"I don't know? Until I have it all done. I can't believe finals are already next week. The time really has flown by already. I want to knock out my final papers that are due in both of my classes before I start studying for the tests."

"Do you want to plan to come have dinner with me sometime this evening? You can sample the new summer beer I tapped yesterday. I think you'll really enjoy it."

"I can make that happen. What time do you want me to come down?"

"Whenever you want. I'm just the extra set of hands on deck, with it being a night we release a new beer. So, whenever you get there, I'll just take a break and have dinner with you. If the bar is full, we can take the food upstairs to the office."

"Sounds like a plan. I'll head up there once I'm done with my work, then. It'll give me something to look forward to."

"You could invite Tiffany and Colton to join, if you wanted?" he suggests.

"Maybe. I might just wait until next weekend to get together with her. Wait until I'm not stressing over school for a little while."

"You stress over school? Pfft. You'd never do something like that," he teases. "Not that you have anything *to* stress over, Miss four-point-oh over here. My girlfriend is a smarty pants, one quality that I find extremely attractive, I want you to know," he adds, pulling me in for a kiss.

"Sometimes I can't help it." I whine a little against his lips.

A devilish grin appears on his face. "I can help with relieving some of that stress."

"I'm sure you can," I say, laughing at his facial expression.

Nick looks at his watch, seeing just how late it has gotten. "Shit. I've got to get going. Don't lose track of time and forget to come eat with me tonight," he says, pushing back from the table and standing. He grabs his plate and empty cup, then bends down to kiss me before he heads inside the house. A few minutes later, I hear the front door close.

I stay on the porch for a few minutes longer, just soaking up the warm day we're having. The sun on my skin feels amazing. So amazing, in fact, that I grab my notebook and laptop from inside, then head back outside and spread my things out on the table. I get to work, finishing up my paper, then start the paper for my second class.

I stop working when Max starts hitting my arm with his nose, not stopping until I give him my undivided attention. I've once again lost track of time, as I was in the zone. I look around and realize the sun has started to set, so that tells me it's getting kinda late. A quick glance at the clock shows it's already a little after seven, so I save my work before powering my computer down, and take everything inside. I get Max fed, then quickly change my clothes into something that is appropriate to wear outside the house, and head for the bar.

As soon as I walk in the back door, I know tonight is another stellar night. I can feel the rumble from the crowd before I see them, and just know the bar is packed again tonight. This is how it's been for months now, especially after Nick started brewing house beers. Ever since that first night back in January, they've kept super busy with the brewery side of things and will be expanding the tank space this summer.

The plan is to eventually add in the equipment to have eight beers going at once. They've continued the Ash and Kat flavors constantly since the start, only rotating out the third option one small batch at a time. People have been flocking to that third flavor, knowing once it's gone, it's gone for good, maybe to return for a special occasion, but it might also not ever make it back into the rotation.

"Hey," I greet Nick as I walk up to the bar.

"You finally made it." He grins as he wipes his hands off on a bar towel before pulling me in for a kiss. "Missed you," he says against my lips, then goes back in for another kiss.

"Missed you, too. Sorry it's late, I lost track of time."

"Again," he teases.

"Again," I reply, a smile of my own cresting my lips as I confirm his suspicion.

"What are you hungry for tonight?" he asks as he lets me go, so he can fill a couple of orders that came in for the new beer.

"I'm thinking a grilled chicken sandwich, but with no bun, sounds good. And extra sauce, please."

He starts punching our order into the computer system. "What do you want for your side?"

"Um, some fruit if they have any." I need to stay away from the fries and such as much as I can if I want to get these few extra pounds off.

"We do." Nick finishes putting in our order and sends it back to the kitchen. "Try this," he says, sliding a small glass with a sample pour of the new beer in it to me.

I pick up the glass and sniff the liquid first. I'm not a huge hop lover, but so far have enjoyed each of the beers Nick's come up with. This one is his take on a summer shandy beer.

"This is really good," I tell him as I finish off the sample.

"Thanks, it appears to be well-received tonight."

"I told you this would all work out. You just had to have faith that it would."

"I know, and your support has helped tremendously. I couldn't have done all this without you." He comes around the bar, then pulls me into his arms and drops his lips to mine.

"You could have, and you would have, even if our paths hadn't crossed. None of your success has had anything to do with me being here."

"You might not have been in the brewery, helping me physically, but the support and encouragement you give me when I'm stressed or trying to figure something out is just as important."

"You do the same for me, putting up with my scatterbrain, between my work and school stress. If anyone in this relationship is thankful for the other, it's me who's thankful for you. You helped me pick my life up when I needed it the most, and I love you for that," I tell him, pushing up on my toes to press my lips against his.

"Food's up." Katie places our plates down on the bar.

"Thanks," we tell her at the same time.

"Let's go upstairs where it's a little more quiet," Nick suggests, then grabs two bottles of water from behind the bar, handing them over to me before he picks up the two plates. I head down the hall and up the stairs to the office, with him on my heels.

"Did you finish your papers?" he asks as we dig in to our food.

"I finished the first one and have the second one pretty much done. Just need to make one final pass over it to see if I need to add anything to it."

"So, tomorrow is finals study time, then?"

"Pretty much. I might meet a few classmates at the library for a few hours to study together, just waiting to see if that pans out. So, if I'm not home when you get up tomorrow, that's probably where I am."

"Okay. You could always have them over to the house if you wanted. It won't bother me."

"That's okay, I wouldn't want to wake you if we were to get loud."

"You know I sleep like the dead. I don't think that y'all could wake me up just from studying."

"You do sleep like the dead," I say on a laugh. "Maybe I'll offer it up as an option and see what they say."

"I'd say I could bring home a couple of growlers of beer, but then I don't think much studying would get done," he jokes.

"Yes, do that. We can enjoy it *after* we finish studying. By then, we'll all need it. I'm sure if I promise free beer, that will get them all to commit."

"Okay, I'll bring some home, then. One growler of each kind work?"

"That should be plenty. We don't need to get hammered," I tell him, looking at him over the rim of my glasses.

"Hey, watch it," he warns. "Looking at me like that will get you into trouble."

"I don't know what you're talking about," I retort. I know he loves it when I wear my glasses, not sure exactly why. I usually only wear them at home, or when my eyes are tired. I left them on since I was so engrossed in my homework today, and didn't see the need to put my contacts in before I left the house.

"Sure, you don't." He smirks. "You going to be awake when I get home tonight?"

I shrug my shoulders. "Don't know. Depends on how late you'll be."

"I'll probably be out of here by midnight."

"I'll probably be asleep by then, but feel free to wake me up. Especially if it's for some sexy time."

"Oh, I'll be waking you up, you can bet your ass on that." He reaches over to grab the edge of the chair I'm on, and pulls it closer to him. "Maybe I should just take you home *now*," he says, before he wraps his hand around the back of my neck, bringing me in for a demanding kiss.

"I'd be okay with that," I tell him once we finally

break our kiss. I was all for christening every room in his house, but I drew a line at having sex in the bar or the office.

"Then let's go," he says, standing and pulling me up. "I'll take care of our plates, then check in with Katie and Zane, who's in charge behind the bar tonight, to let them know I'm leaving."

"Sounds good. I'll meet you at home, then," I say with a wink before I head down the stairs and out to the parking lot.

I make it home about ten minutes later to a hyper Max. He's always excited when we return home. "Who's a good boy?" I rub the top of his head, and he settles at my feet. "Were you good enough for a treat?" I ask him and his tail starts to tap wildly against the floor. I walk over to the counter where we have the jar of treats for him and grab one out.

"Come here," I tell him, heading into the living room. "Sit." I point to the floor in front of me. "Good boy. Now, shake," I instruct, holding out my hand, and he places his paw into it for me to shake. "You're such a good boy."

I drop his paw, then hold up the treat in my hand, showing it to him, and he patiently waits for the cue that he can take it from my hand. "Okay," I finally tell him, and he gently reaches forward and takes it from me.

"I'm home," Nick calls out as he walks through the door. Max jumps up and barks excitedly at him, running over to greet him. "Hey, boy. You being good today?" he asks, scratching him on the head.

"Don't let him fool you, he just finished a treat."

"You wouldn't do that, would you, boy?" he coos, scratching Max's belly now, as he lies on the floor at Nick's feet.

Laughing, I say, "You know he would."

"He's only convinced us he needed a treat about every day he's been ours," Nick agrees.

"Did Katie or Zane give you any issues with leaving a little early?"

"Nope, they had everything under control. Justin was also behind the bar with Zane, and Jessa is out on the floor with Katie, so we're well-covered."

"Good. I'd feel bad if you left for me when they needed your help."

"I wouldn't have left if they needed me, even with the promise of you naked in our bed, as much as it would've pained me. I'd have stayed until close, if that's what I needed to do. But they're good, I'm here, and now I get to finish what we started earlier." Nick pulls me into his arms and brings his lips to my neck, running the tip of his nose up and down my skin, which causes my skin to break out in goose bumps. A shiver travels down my spine, setting my core on fire.

Nick reaches for the hem of my shirt, grasping it in his hands as he slides them up my sides, and lifts my shirt up and over my head. I can see the desire, the love he has for me, shining in his eyes as they drop from my own, down my body. He's definitely a breast man, and takes no time at all before he's burying his face between mine. With my bra on, they're still well on display and creating the perfect amount of cleavage for him to play in.

"God, I love your nipples." He pulls the cup of my left breast down and laps at said nipple. "They're so responsive to my tongue," he says between licks, each one causing my nipples to harden even more.

"I love your mouth on them," I tell him in encouragement as he sucks my nipple back into his mouth, working me over. My back arches, pressing my chest even further into his grasp. He releases the one breast, moving over to deliver the same attention to my other one. He's on his knees in front of me and still able to be eye level with my chest.

As he flicks my nipple with his tongue, I feel his hand slip around my side and onto my back, until he finds the clasp of my bra. He makes quick work of the clasp and removes it from my arms as he worships my breasts, cupping one with his hand while the other is still in his mouth. He rolls my nipple between his fingers while his tongue flicks the other, driving me insane.

"I need you," I whine, trying my best to get his shirt off of him.

"You need to be patient," he tells me, a wolfish smirk on his lips as he looks up at me from his position in front of me. His hands travel down my sides, sliding around to my back and down to my ass, which he cups and squeezes.

"I don't want to be patient," I pout, knowing damn well if I am, he'll give me so much pleasure.

"Oh, but you do," he says, as he skims his lips across my stomach. He makes quick work of my shorts and panties and before I know it, I'm standing in front of him, completely naked and on display for his liking. His eyes flash with desire as he looks his fill, licking his lips as if he's about to devour his favorite meal.

"God, you're beautiful and I'm one lucky ass man," he murmurs before pressing his lips to my skin, just above my pubic bone. He sits back on his haunches, pulling me along with him, then lifts one of my legs and tosses it over his shoulder.

Nick starts to plant kisses along my inner thigh and my body trembles with anticipation the moment his tongue makes contact with my clit. He licks up my seam, parting my folds with his tongue as he circles it around my clit, driving me crazy with lust as my orgasm builds. He slips two fingers inside me, thrusting in rhythm with the movement of his tongue.

"Gah!" I cry out. "I'm going to come!" I warn him as I feel my orgasm barrel through my body. I slide my fingers into his hair, pulling a little hard, as my body shakes. My release builds and finally crests over the edge, into pure bliss.

Nick pulls his fingers from my body and pushes himself up to stand while I do my best to keep from falling over from the intensity of my orgasm. He quickly picks me up in his arms, bridal style, and takes us down the hall to our bedroom. He places me on the bed, then quickly sheds his own clothes.

"About time you got naked with me," I tease.

"Ready for round two?" he asks, hovering over me as I lay back on the bed.

"For you, yes. I need you inside me. I need to feel how large your cock is. I want to ride it until I come again," I tell him boldly. He's the only partner I've had where I've felt comfortable enough to actually tell him what I want, and how I want it. It took a bit of time to get to this point, but as Nick gained not only my heart but my love and soul, I've done my best to open up to him, just as he has with me.

"Move up some," he commands, his lips against my neck once again.

I slide up the bed until my head reaches the pillows.

"You ready for me?" he asks, rolling a condom down his shaft. He taps the head of his cock against my clit a few times, then rubs it through my folds, spreading my own wetness around my sex.

"Yes," I gasp as he presses his cock against my clit. The sensation has me ready to detonate.

I watch as he holds his cock in one hand, the other holding his weight. He taps my clit one last time, then lines himself up with my entrance. One second later, he's buried deep inside of me and I feel his tip hit my g-spot.

"God, yes!" I shout once he's seated, stilling to allow my body to adjust to his size.

"You feel like heaven, baby," he whispers against my ear as he starts to pull out before pushing back in. He starts his thrusts out slow and sensual, pulling out, then sliding back in slowly. Each time he pushes back in, he makes contact with my clit, adding just enough pressure to make my eyes roll back in my head.

"I'm not going to last long," I warn as he starts to pick up his thrusts, finding a fast pace as he pounds me into an explosive orgasm. My back bows off the bed, my breaths ragged, short gasps, as I try and take in enough air while my body goes limp from my release.

Nick slows down, slipping from me as my body basks in the glory that is sex hormones. Oxytocin and endorphins are firing on all cylinders from the two orgasms I've had so far tonight. "What are you doing?" I ask, when I realize he's sprawled on the bed, just staring me down.

"I'm waiting on you to ride my cock," he says bluntly, his own hand shuttling up and down his shaft as he keeps himself aroused and hard. I take his cue and climb on top of him, straddling his hips. His cock slides easily through my folds, hitting my clit with each pass. "No more playing," Nick promises, gripping his cock as he lines it up as I sink down on top of it. I ride him, quickly bringing us both close to the edge.

"Need you with me," he grits out, bringing his thumb to my clit to help me crest over. He grips my hip, thrusting upwards as I come back down. That's all it takes to set both of us off. He grunts as he explodes into the condom.

I collapse forward, resting my forehead against his shoulder. Nick runs his hands along my back as we both melt into the bed, enjoying the endorphins as they flood our body after our respective orgasms.

"Love you," he whispers against my ear as I start to nod off.

"Love you."

I feel him move me off of him, then feel the bed dip as he rolls off and heads into the bathroom. He returns a minute later, and slides back into bed next to me, wrapping me in his arms as he settles in with me.

I melt into him, already half-asleep, my thoughts on the future and how much has changed in my life since I met this amazing man I get to call mine. The one who picked my life up when it was on the ground. Saved me from myself when I was in a downward spiral. The one who showed me I just needed to learn to love myself before I could allow someone else to love me just as much. He's shown me what a real man is like. How a real man can love the woman in his life more than life itself.

EPILOGUE
NICK

Four Years Later

"Are you ready?" I ask Ashley as she stands in front of the full-length mirror in our bathroom, attaching her graduation cap with some bobby pins.

"I will be in just a minute," she says, smiling at me in the reflection.

"You look perfect, babe. And that cap isn't going anywhere," I tell her on a chuckle.

"Well, I don't want it to slip while I'm walking."

"You're going to have it so well-secured to your head, you won't be able to get it off your head when it's time to toss it into the air with your class."

"Then I guess I won't toss it," she says, sticking her tongue out at me. She slides in another pin, then turns to face me. "How do I look?"

"Like a bombshell," I tell her honestly. "I'm so

fucking proud of you."

I pull her into my arms and wrap them around her, tugging her close as I bury my face into her neck, then breathe her in. Her perfume fills my lungs and with her body pressed so close to mine, my cock hardens in my slacks.

"No time for that. We've got to go, and you're *not* messing up my hair," she chides, pulling back slightly from my hold on her.

"Later," I tell her, nipping at her lips.

"Later," she agrees, and the desire she has for me flashes in her eyes. It's hard for me to believe we've been together for almost five years already.

We've supported each other through everything, from growing pains at the bar and brewery, to her hectic work and school schedule, and everything else that has come our way over the years. This woman is the best thing to ever happen to me, and I can't wait to celebrate her accomplishment today.

Then, later tonight, I hope to be celebrating her agreeing to be with me for the rest of our lives. For her to agree to take my last name and hopefully one day give us kids. I've already got the ring hidden in the center console of my truck, where I'll be able to easily grab it after dinner, when I'm ready to propose.

"All right, let's get out of here. I've got seats to save for everyone," I tell her as we exit the bathroom.

"You be a good boy," Ashley tells Max as he lays down on his bed in the living room. His age is catching up to him, and we're watching him closely these days to make sure he isn't suffering.

"Ready?" I ask, holding the door open for her.

"Ready." She grabs her purse and heads to the truck.

"Your mom texted me earlier to let me know that David will be coming with her. He was able to get the day off. So, you'll have another person cheering for you when you cross that stage."

Donna met David almost two years ago now, and they've been dating ever since. She finally moved out of that old rundown apartment she lived in for so long, and into David's small house. They've been great for each other and he's treated her well. The way a man *should* treat a woman.

"Oh good. It will be nice to see him. I love that my mom is so happy these days."

"Me too, she deserves the best," I agree. Just like my girl deserves the best, so does her mother. They're both badass women, who have more strength than any man I know. Each of them has lived through things no person should have to, but they've both come out the other side stronger. Life might have handed them lemons, but they definitely made lemonade, maybe even with a splash of rum in it.

"What time is everyone planning to meet you?" she asks. Since she has to arrive almost two hours early, I told our family I would just go with her and save us some seats, so they didn't have to show up as early.

"I think about a half an hour or so before start time. Kaiden said they went ahead and got a babysitter, so Thomas won't be with them."

"Probably a smart idea. Tiffany was planning on the same thing for Lucy."

"Yeah, she texted me, as well, to let me know it would be just her and Colton. So, I'll be grabbing nine seats, at last count."

"Hopefully, no one gives you a hard time about it," she says, straightening her dress as I drive down the road toward the campus.

"I don't think anyone will, and if they have a problem with it, they can get the fuck over it."

I WHISTLE AS LOUD AS I CAN AS ASHLEY'S NAME IS called, and she walks gracefully across the stage. Our entire row is standing as she turns and smiles at the crowd. She looks directly this way, a huge smile on her lips as she slides her tassel from one side to the other then walks off the stage. I watch her as she returns to her seat, so fucking proud of everything she's accomplished over the last few years.

And she's not done yet.

She's already been accepted into the Master's program, and will be dropping back to part-time at the clinic, to accommodate her class schedule when classes start back up in the fall. The clinic has already offered her a counselor position once she completes her Master's. They're also paying for it, as part of her employment contract. She agreed to work for them for a minimum of five years, and they pay for the entire Master's program, upfront.

"You did it! I'm so proud of you!" Donna tells her, once the ceremony is finally over and Ashley has reached our group. She makes her way through all our family and friends, accepting hugs and flowers from everyone. I'm the last person she makes it to, and as soon as she's in my arms, my lips find hers.

"I love you," I say against her lips. "And I'm so fucking proud of you."

"Love you, too, and thank you. I couldn't have done this without you."

"You could have, but I'll let you think differently."

"Are you guys ready to get out of here?" my mom asks, pulling us from our intimate moment.

"Yes! I'm starving," Ashley says, taking off her graduation gown. She leaves the cap right now, since it's so securely attached to her head with the number of pins she used earlier. I'll help her remove it before dinner.

"Our reservations are in about forty-five minutes, so we should make it to the restaurant in perfect time," my dad states, looking at his watch.

"Then let's get out of here. Does everyone know where we're headed?" I ask our group.

"We've got it in the GPS," Tiffany says, and everyone else nods their heads.

"I'd like to make a toast," Donna says a short while later, once everyone has been served their drinks and our appetizer orders have been placed with the server.

"Ash," she says, then stops for a moment, already holding back tears as her emotions take over. "I'm so proud of you. For everything you've been through, for how you found resilience, how you figured out how to pick your life back up after you'd been knocked down, time and time again. You never gave up on your dream and look at where it has you today.

"I'm so thankful you found such a wonderful man to love you, and to show you that you deserve to be loved. I might have learned a thing or two about that, from his example." She nods to me and then to David. "Most of all, I'm proud of the woman you are today. I love you and I wish nothing but the best for you. Cheers," she finishes, lifting her glass slightly higher, signaling everyone to take a drink.

"I love you so much, Mom," Ashley says, standing to hug her mom. They both lose their fight to hold back the tears as they hold on to one another.

With the tears out of the way, we all tell stories and allow the conversation to flow, along with the wine, throughout the meal.

With the tables cleared of our dinner plates, it's finally time for me to pop the question. Everyone at the table except for Ashley knows what's about to go down. I slipped the ring box to my dad when we got to the restaurant, so he could hold it for me until I needed it. When Ashley excused herself to the bathroom at the end of our main course, he handed it to me.

I stand, and pull her up with me.

"Ash." I pause to clear my own throat as *my* emotions hit me, and I see the tears start to pool along her lashes when I drop to one knee.

"Nick," she gasps, covering her mouth with one hand as what I'm about to do hits her.

"Ash, from the first moment I saw you crying in a booth in my bar, to the moment I kissed you in my bathroom, to the moment we moved in together, and all the other amazing moments we've shared over the last few years, to our amazing life together now. You've brought so much into my life, and I don't ever want that to change. Would you do me the honor of being my wife?"

"Yes!" she cries out, bending over to say it over and over again against my lips. I wrap my arms around her waist as I stand back up, gathering her against my body as I seal my lips over hers. I vaguely hear the cheers from our family and friends as I get lost in my new fiancée.

"Can I have my ring?" she finally asks, as we pull back from each other. It's then I realize I never slid it on her finger in my haste to pick her up and get my mouth on her. I slide the diamond ring I picked out a few months ago onto her ring finger.

"Do you like it?" I ask, nervous she isn't going to.

"It's perfect," she says, looking at it, then back up at me.

"I love you." I bring my lips back to hers for another chaste kiss.

"Not as much as I love you," she tells me once we break our connection.

"That's debatable," I say on a laugh. "We can argue that fact for the rest of our lives. How's that sound?"

"Sounds perfect."

***

Looking for more books inspired by the Lyrics of songs?
Find more Lyrics and Love books on your favorite retailer!
Marry Me
Rumor Going 'Round

***

I HOPE YOU HAVE ENJOYED THIS BOOK, AND YOU would consider leaving a review on your favorite retailer.

If you would like to connect more with Samantha, please join her reader group on Facebook!

COMING SOON

To find out what's next from Samantha, please visit her website at samanthalind.com

ALSO BY SAMANTHA LIND

INDIANAPOLIS EAGLES SERIES

Just Say Yes ~ Scoring The Player

Playing For Keeps ~ Protecting Her Heart

Against The Boards ~ The First Intermission

The Hardest Shot ~ The Game Changer

Rookie Move ~ The Final Period

Box Set 1 {Books 1-3} ~ Box Set 2 {Books 4-6}

Box Set 3 {Books 7-10}

INDIANAPOLIS LIGHTNING SERIES

The Perfect Pitch ~ The Curve Ball

The Screw Ball ~ The Change Up

LYRICS & LOVE SERIES

Marry Me ~ Drunk Girl

Rumor Going 'Round ~ Just A Kiss

STANDALONE TITLES

Tempting Tessa

Then You Came Along

When I Found You

Cocky Doc

SWEET VALLEY, TENNESSEE

Nothing Bundt Love

Nothing Bundt Forever

San Francisco Shockwaves

Ryker ~ Aiden ~ Tristan

Damien ~ Blake

Austin Fusion

Zack

ACKNOWLEDGMENTS

Thank you to my family! I love you all!

Thank you to my team! Y'all are amazing!

Thanks to Melissa Gill Designs for the amazingly beautiful cover! I fell in love with this cover the moment I saw it for the first time; I just had to wait for the perfect book to use it for!

Taylor Alexander Photography ~ Thank you for the beautiful image and for all the support!

Give Me Books & the bloggers!!! THANK YOU FOR EVERYTHING YOU DO! You are all amazing, and I love each and every one of you! Thank you for pimping out my books, for every post, tag, and time you recommend any of my books means the world to me!

READERS! You are really the rock stars here! And I leave you for last to thank, because as the saying goes: You leave the best for last! THANK YOU SO MUCH FOR EVERYTHING! If it wasn't for you loving my words and buying my books, telling your friends about them, sharing them on your social media etc., I wouldn't be able to do this. So once again, I thank you from the bottom of my heart!

Xoxo
Samantha

ABOUT THE AUTHOR

Samantha Lind is a *USA TODAY* Bestselling contemporary romance author. When she's not dreaming up new stories, she can often be found with her family, traveling, reading, watching her boys on the ice or watching her favorite professional team (Go Knights Go!).

Connect with Samantha in the following places:
www.samanthalind.com
samantha@samanthalind.com

Reader Group
Samantha Lind's Alpha Loving Ladies
Good Reads
https://goo.gl/t3R9Vm
Newsletter
https://bit.ly/FDSLNL

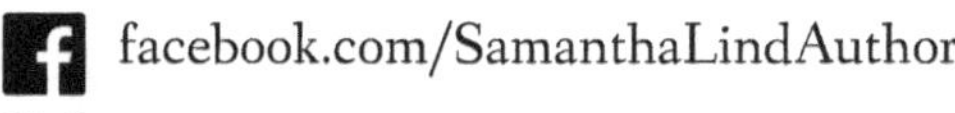

facebook.com/SamanthaLindAuthor
x.com/samanthalind1
instagram.com/samanthalindauthor
bookbub.com/authors/samantha-lind